I0608608

MYRA'S DAUGHTERS

A Novel

"We never see our parents as they really are. They are always our parents, figures of authority in the landscape of our childhood who have control of us and can punish us for our wrongdoings. All our lives we strive for their love and approval and are never sure that we have it."

Also by Muriel Maddox

Noela
That Man in Rio
Captain from Corfu
Love and Betrayal
Llantarnam

MYRA'S
DAUGHTERS

MYRA'S DAUGHTERS

A Novel
by
Muriel Maddox

SUNSTONE
PRESS

This book is a work of fiction. Names, characters, places and incidents are either products of the author's imagination or are used fictitiously. Any resemblance to actual events or locales or persons, living or dead, is entirely coincidental.

© 2001 by Muriel Maddox. All rights reserved.

Printed and bound in the United States of America. No part of this book may be reproduced in any form or by any electronic or mechanical means including information storage and retrieval systems without permission in writing from the publisher, except by a reviewer who may quote brief passages in a review.

Sunstone books may be purchased for educational, business, or sales promotional use. For information please write: Special Markets Department, Sunstone Press, P.O. Box 2321, Santa Fe, New Mexico 87504-2321.

Library of Congress Cataloging-in-Publication Data:
Maddox, Muriel,
    Myra's daughters: a novel / by Muriel Maddox.—1st ed.
        p. cm
    ISBN: 978-0-86534-323-8 (hardcover) ISBN: 978-1-63293-126-9 (softcover)
    1. Washington (D.C.)—Fiction. 2. Mothers and daughters—Fiction.
        3. Sisters—Fiction I. Title.
    PS3563.A339455 M97 2001
    813'.54—dc21   2001020181

Published by SUNSTONE PRESS
                Post Office Box 2321
                Santa Fe, NM 87504-2321 / USA
                (505) 988-4418 / orders only (800) 243-5644
                FAX (505) 988-1025
                www.sunstonepress.com

For Blake and Evan

O what a tangled web we weave
When first we practice to deceive!

—Sir Walter Scott

PROLOGUE

IN THE SEPIA PHOTOGRAPH she is seated on a high-backed brocade sofa looking wistfully and expectantly at the camera, a faint smile on her lips. Of what is she dreaming, my mother, so long ago, before she was married, before life disappointed her? Her dress is of filmy chiffon with a lace bodice caught at the waist with a silken rose and trailing satin ribbons. Her feet in pale satin pumps are crossed at the ankles and around her neck is a single strand of pearls. A ring sparkles on her engagement finger. Could it be her engagement picture? I don't know. I found it in a trunk when I was going through things after she died.

All her life she took pride in her naturally curly hair and her narrow feet. Her name was Myra and she lived until she was ninety-eight. But how could she have known the lengthy life span ahead of her as she sat for her photograph?

Now that Mother is gone, and it is still hard to realize it, I try to imagine her life, to separate her from my mother and see her as a woman.

We seldom see our parents as they really are. They are always our parents, figures of authority in the landscape of our childhood who have control of us and can punish us for our wrong-doings. All our lives we strive for their love and approval and are never sure that we have it.

And it does not end when they die. . . .

1

WHEN SHE WAS SIX YEARS OLD Annabel wrote her name with a red crayon in large block letters on the pale green cushions of the patio furniture that Mother had just recovered. Mother was furious when she discovered it but Daddy didn't even spank her.

"Well, Annabel," he said, "how nice that you've learned to write your name. But in future will you please write it on your blackboard or on a piece of paper and not on the furniture."

"I didn't do it, Daddy," Annabel insisted. "I didn't!"

Who would have dreamed that fifty years later Annabel would forge Mother's will?

Rooms of my childhood haunt my dreams, I walk through every one and it is as if I am back there touching the old familiar things, like some safe haven stored in my memory, that nothing has changed when everything has. The houses have other owners now, different furniture, yet why do I see everything in detail as if they await my return?

I will never return to any of them, that is my past now, the doors are closed, the key is turned. Yet they remain, still they remain.

My bedroom in the house in Washington on the third floor looking out into the tulip trees that were bare all winter, the twin beds of green metal with flowers painted on the headboards, the mahogany bureau with the lace runner and silver dresser set, the radiators under the windows hissing on chilly mornings when I dressed for school.

The children's rooms were on the third floor, mine and Annabel's, and one for the governess and the cook. Mother and Daddy slept in separate rooms on the second floor and there were two other bedrooms which were for guests, like when Grandfather and Grandmother came to visit from Pittsburgh or other relatives and friends.

I knew little of the outside world and I believed that everyone lived like that.

Out of our beginnings emerge the adults we become later in life, and I keep going over and over in my mind my childhood memories of Annabel, like the picture puzzles I used to do on rainy days, I try to fit the pieces together, but they don't fit. Annabel, my sister. How could she do what she did? Did she not realize the consequences of her act, or did she honestly believe it was justified?

Daddy always admired the poems of Edgar Allan Poe and Annabel was named after one of his favorites, "Annabel Lee." Sometimes after he had had a few bourbons I would hear him reciting it in the library. I think he wanted to be a poet, but that wasn't practical so he became a stockbroker instead. He came from a romantic city, Charleston, and when I was small and went to visit my other grandparents there, the Ashfords, I remember ornately-carved gates in front of the houses and the sweet scent of jasmine and the salt-air smell of the sea.

For Mother, no man ever lived up to her father, Henry Calhoun, the steel magnate from Pittsburgh, who had started with nothing as a young man in Glasgow, Scotland. Poor Daddy. All the money we had came from the Calhouns but Daddy said we got our good name from the Ashfords. It was a strange marriage of two totally different people.

I am five years old and I am waiting at the top of the stairs, peering eagerly through the spokes of the railing for Uncle Edgar to arrive for a visit from New York. He is Mother's younger brother and my favorite uncle. I have on a new dress, pale blue with smocking and a lace collar and high white socks and white shoes with bows and a strap around the ankle. My knee has a big scab where I tripped and fell in the garden last week. I keep trying not to pick it off and make it bleed again because that will only take it longer to heal, Mother tells me, but it is difficult. I am always getting scratches and scabs and I want to look nice for Uncle Edgar and I hope he will not notice. He is so wonderful! Mother says he is off now on a trip to South America with a friend. I wonder who the friend is and I am jealous.

Suddenly I hear a bustle downstairs. The front door has opened, and Mother and the chauffeur have returned from meeting Uncle Edgar at Union Station.

"Where's Barbara?" I hear his voice. "Is she hiding someplace?"

"Uncle Edgar, Uncle Edgar!" I run down the stairs, almost tripping on a step in my eagerness to see him and, yes, let's be honest, like all small children to see what he has brought me.

He has put down his suitcase and is holding a large, gaily-wrapped package.

"From F.A.O. Schwarz. Oh, Edgar, you shouldn't, you'll spoil her," Mother says, as I throw myself into Uncle Edgar's arms and he gives me a bear hug.

"Nothing's too good for my favorite niece," he says.

I rip open the package eagerly. It contains a doll, the most beautiful doll I have ever seen. She has a china face and blue eyes and long golden curls. I am speechless.

"What do you say?" Mother asks.

I hang my head shyly. I am embarrassed. Why is everyone watching me?

"She loves the doll, Edgar," Mother says. "Don't you, Barbara?"

I hold the doll in my arms. She is mine. Mine. "Oh, yes. Thank you, Uncle Edgar."

Uncle Edgar is so handsome. He seemed tall to me then, but he was of medium height with soft brown eyes and dark curly hair. His eyes, though, have something sad about them and I wonder why. Later, years later, I recognized that look. It was the look of tragedy.

The floors smell of fresh wax and the scent of apples and cinnamon wafts from the kitchen. "Lavinia has baked an apple pie for you, Edgar," Mother says.

"My favorite." Uncle Edgar smacks his lips in anticipation. I love apple pie too. The smell makes me hungry. I hope we aren't having sweetbreads or something awful like that for dinner, as I know I won't be allowed any dessert if I don't clean my plate. "Think of all the starving children in China who would be happy to have this," Mother is always reminding me.

Dinner was roast chicken with stuffing and rice and lima beans. I pushed my lima beans around my plate, hoping that no one would notice that I wasn't eating them while I listened to the grown-ups talk. Daddy was saying something about the stock market to Uncle Edgar and Mother was listening intently with a worried expression.

"Do you really think we're going to have a depression, Lamont?" Mother asked. "Father doesn't think so. He says the steel business has never been better."

Daddy looked annoyed. "Your father—" he started, then stopped.

"Well, I'm sure Edgar wouldn't be going on this cruise," Mother continued, "if the economy was in as dire straits as you predict."

"Are you going on a big boat, Uncle Edgar?" I asked.

Uncle Edgar smiled. "A pretty big boat, Barbara. I'll be sailing all around South America." And I listened in awe to names like Rio de Janeiro and Buenos Aires and Santiago.

"I'd like to go to all those places," I said. "Will you take me one day?"

"When you're bigger I will," he promised. "And I'll send you picture postcards from my trip."

Mother was looking at my lima beans pushed in a corner of my plate under my knife and fork. Please don't make me eat them!

"And you'll have to tell me all about the Inauguration Parade," Uncle Edgar said.

"I certainly hope things are better under Herbert Hoover than they've been with Calvin Coolidge," Daddy said.

"At least Al Smith didn't get elected," said Uncle Edgar.

"No chance of a Catholic ever being President," Daddy said.

I didn't understand all of this conversation but I was looking forward to the parade next month. I loved parades and Daddy told me we were going to sit in a grandstand opposite the White House so we would have a good view of everything.

Lavinia came in and removed the plates and brought in the dessert plates. They had pink and lavender flowers on them and were trimmed in gold. I guess Mother had decided not to make a scene about the lima beans because Uncle Edgar was here and I was glad. Lavinia served the apple pie. Dessert was always my favorite part of the meal.

"I see you've inherited my sweet tooth," Uncle Edgar said. "And your grandmother's pretty blue-gray eyes. Doesn't Barbara look like pictures of Mother as a child, Myra?"

"Yes, I see what you mean."

"You're going to be a beautiful woman when you grow up."

Uncle Edgar always made me feel so good. I wish he could come and stay with us more often.

"But Barbara didn't inherit my curly hair," Mother said, and I immediately felt deflated. Why couldn't she pay me compliments like Uncle Edgar?

"Where do I come in in all this?" Daddy asked.

"She has your chin, Lamont," Mother said. "Stubborn."

"Let's go to the zoo tomorrow," said Uncle Edgar. "Would you like that, Barbara?"

"Oh, yes!" I clapped my hands in delight.

"Good. Then I'll take you." He turned to Mother. "I know Lamont will be at his brokerage office, but would you like to join us?"

"You two go together, Edgar. I've got some shopping I have to do."

And so the visit with Uncle Edgar passed quickly and then he was gone back to New York to board the big white ship and sail away. Perhaps the reason I remember it all so vividly is because it was the last time I was ever to see Uncle Edgar.

Inauguration Day, March 4, 1929. It was a bitter cold wintry morning with snow flurries in the air. I was all bundled up in my blue coat with leggings and a hat with ear flaps and mittens, but my hands and feet were still cold and my nose felt like an icicle attached to my face. The parade went on for hours and I had to go to the bathroom but there was no place to go and I thought it would never end.

"When you are grown up you can say that you attended the inauguration of Herbert Hoover," Daddy said, but all I cared about was going to the bathroom.

When we got back to our house on Tracy Place, Lavinia was waiting for us. She had a yellow Western Union telegram on the silver tray Mother used for calling cards and Mother looked alarmed when Lavinia handed it to her, but I didn't wait to see what it was all about as I ran for the nearest bathroom, the powder room off the front hall. While I was sitting on the toilet I heard Mother scream.

"Oh no, my God, no! It can't be true. I don't believe it!" Mother cried and then there were sobs as I hurried as fast as I could to see what was wrong.

Daddy was trying to console Mother who was crying and holding the crumpled telegram in her hand. Lavinia had brought a bottle of brandy and a glass and Daddy poured some and tried to get Mother to drink it but she pushed it away.

"Edgar!" A terrible moan came from her, the most awful sound I had ever heard. "My baby brother." She held out the telegram to Daddy. "Tell me it's not true, Lamont."

I started to tremble. Uncle Edgar. Something had happened to my Uncle Edgar. Something awful. Lavinia took hold of me. "Come upstairs, child."

I pulled away. "No. I want to know what is wrong."

"Go upstairs with Lavinia," Daddy said, and she led me away, up to the third floor to my room and she closed the door and her black face looked very sad.

"You will be glad one day that you had the nice visit with your Uncle Edgar," she said. "Because now he has gone away forever."

Still I did not understand, but it had something to do with the yellow telegram that had brought the terrible news.

"What did the telegram say?" I asked.

"It was from your grandfather. Your uncle has been lost at sea. He has been drowned."

I imagined Uncle Edgar disappearing into the ocean, the blue-green water covering his curly hair, foam in his face as he sank slowly from sight. I started to cry and Lavinia put her arms around me.

"There, there, baby. Your Uncle Edgar is with the good Lord in heaven now with all the angels."

"Does he have wings and a halo?"

"I'm sure he does, honey. He was a kind man."

"But I want to see him. Won't I ever see him again?"

"One day. When we all enter the Pearly Gates."

I didn't know what Lavinia meant by the Pearly Gates, all I knew was that my beloved Uncle Edgar had been drowned and I wouldn't see him for a long, long time. "I don't feel well," I said. "My tummy hurts."

"You get into bed, honey lamb, and Lavinia will bring you some milk toast." She pulled back the covers and handed me my nightgown. "Do you want me to help you undress?"

"No, I can do it myself."

I got into bed and lay there looking out the window at the bare trees. It was snowing now and I shivered thinking of Uncle Edgar going down, down in the cold ocean, not able to get any air. Did he know he was drowning and did he struggle to save himself? Across the room the doll he had given me stared back and I thought I saw tears in her eyes.

It was my first experience with death, but it would be far from my last.

2

MOTHER LOOKED DIFFERENTwhen she came back from Uncle Edgar's funeral in Pittsburgh. She was wearing black with a black hat and a long black veil and black stockings. I snuggled against her fur coat and smelled her perfume, lily of the valley, and she held me longer than she usually did. I stroked her face and tried to comfort her as I saw tears roll down her cheek. She was very pale. "My little Barbara," she said. "You loved him too."

"Lavinia says we'll see Uncle Edgar when we go through the Pearly Gates," I said, thinking this would make her feel better, but it only made her cry more.

"He left you something special," Mother said through her sobs.

Uncle Edgar had thought of me even when he was drowning? Or perhaps he had sent it from where the Pearly Gates were. He had flown through the sky with his brand-new wings and left it for me.

"A present?" I asked.

"Kind of," Mother said. "But you won't get it for a long time."

"Why not?"

"Because he left you something in his will," Daddy said. "And you only get it after all the Calhouns . . ." He stopped. "You won't get it for a long time. But one day you'll be a very rich woman."

"I'd like to lie down, Lamont," Mother said. "I'm not feeling well."

"Of course, darling. It's been a tiring trip. I'll ask Lavinia to make you some tea."

Grown-ups talked about so many things I didn't understand, I thought, as Daddy helped Mother up the stairs. And they didn't seem very happy. I wanted to stay a child for as long as I could.

You wonder where Annabel is in all this? She is not here yet, but she will be soon. For Annabel was born out of tragedy. "I always felt that I was a mistake," she told me in later years. "That Mother didn't really want me."

Was that to excuse the things she did? So that nothing ever filled the void, no matter how much she had? But I can't excuse her, because what she did hurt so many people. It was greedy and callous and cruel.

Mother dresses in black all the time now and her eyes are red from weeping. I miss the pretty colors she used to wear, especially blue to match her eyes. She is very thin and scarcely eats anything. I want to remind her of all the starving children in China but I don't think she would like it. We are all worried about her. Lavinia tries to tempt her with new dishes but she pushes them away.

Finally Daddy loses patience with her. "Myra, it won't bring Edgar back for you to make yourself ill."

"I can't help it. Why? I keep asking myself over and over again, why did he do it? For what reason?"

Daddy threw a quick glance at me and then back at Mother. "This is not the place to discuss it."

What did they mean? And what wasn't I supposed to know? I would ask Lavinia.

Lavinia came in with Brown Betty, one of my very favorite desserts, sliced apples with brown sugar and all crispy on top. I could hardly wait to taste it, but Mother just shook her head as Lavinia passed it to her.

"Mrs. Ashford, please try just a little bit. You don't eat hardly enough to keep a bird alive."

"Yes, Myra," Daddy added. "Lavinia will think you don't like her cooking anymore."

"Just a tiny bit," Mother said.

"And some hard sauce?" Without waiting for an answer, Lavinia put some on Mother's plate.

"I love Apple Betty," I said, helping myself to a big portion.

"Yes, we never have trouble with you with dessert," Daddy said. "I wished you liked vegetables as well."

Mother took two bites of her Apple Betty and then said, "I don't feel well. I'm going to bed."

Daddy went upstairs with her and I went in the kitchen to see Lavinia, taking my empty plate with me. Lavinia was fixing coffee.

"Can I have more Apple Betty? Please?"

"I'll bring it in the dining room. With the coffee."

"But they've all left. Mother felt sick again and Daddy went with her." I sat down at the kitchen table covered in yellow oilcloth with blue flowers and traced the design with my finger. "Lavinia, I want to ask you something."

"You know your mother doesn't want you sitting in the kitchen with the help."

"Why not?"

"She just doesn't." Lavinia dished out a portion of Apple Betty and I gobbled it down. I had almost forgotten what I wanted to ask her about Uncle Edgar and then she shook her head and said, "Poor lady," and I remembered.

"Lavinia, what is it they don't want to tell me? It's something about Uncle Edgar, isn't it?"

Lavinia's black face looked serious, but she pretended to be busy with the coffee, putting two cups with saucers on a silver tray with the silver sugar bowl and creamer.

"What is it?"

"Hush, child. Your Daddy wouldn't want me talking about it with you." She glanced nervously up the back stairs, as if she expected Daddy to come down any minute. "You go up to your room and play and I'll see you in a little while."

I went upstairs and colored pictures with my crayons until Lavinia came in and told me that Mother wanted me to take my bath and get ready for bed and then Daddy would tuck me in and read me a story. I asked her how Mother was feeling and Lavinia just shrugged her shoulders. "It'll take her a while," she said. "Come, let's run your bath."

Strange, from earliest childhood I never remember calling my mother anything but Mother. Never Mama, though I probably said that as a baby when I first started to talk, but of course I don't remember that. I used to wish she would hug and kiss me more and tell me that she loved me, but I guess that wasn't her way and it was hard for her to express her feelings. I was never really sure until the very end when she lay dying in the hospital, a tube in her nose and one arm strapped to the metal railing of the bed, that she struggled to say the words: "I love you very much."

My first memory is of visiting my Aunt Edith at her house in Winston-Salem. Aunt Edith was twelve years older than Mother and was very thin with shallow skin and wore no lipstick the way Mother did, just a bit of powder on her nose so it wouldn't shine. She always dressed in a plain but very expensive wool or silk dress with a large diamond bar pin at her throat. My cousin Jean had a beautiful rocking horse and I wanted so much to ride it but she wouldn't let me. She wouldn't let me play with her dollhouse either. Mother said later that Jean was selfish, just like Aunt Edith.

We went to a pond afterwards and I fed the ducks some dried bread. I liked feeding the ducks and I wanted to take one home with me and put it in my bathtub. Daddy said no.

Mother is sick every morning right after breakfast and the doctor has been coming to see her. I hear him tell her that she must try to walk and get some fresh air, instead of lying in bed so much. It is important for the baby.

The baby? What are they talking about?

I was not supposed to be listening at the door so I don't dare ask.

Grandfather is coming to visit us for several days. He has business to attend to in Washington, Mother says. She is still wearing black and when I ask her how long she is going to dress in black she says for a year in memory of Uncle Edgar. I wonder if the baby will have to wear black too? Daddy told me that I will be having a new brother or sister around Thanksgiving, and he seems happy about it. Mother has gained weight, but she looks very sad all the time.

Daddy says if I am very good and eat all my lunch, I can go with them this afternoon to Union Station to meet Grandfather's train from Pittsburgh. I just hope we won't have eggplant or something I don't like!

The train is pulling into the station and I hold Daddy's hand as he says I must not get too close to the tracks. I love to come to Union Station and see the trains but I like even better to go on one and have the Pullman porter make up the seats into a bed and to eat in the dining car. People are rushing around and porters are pushing carts with luggage.

"There he is," Mother says and waves. "Father!"

Grandfather is carrying one suitcase and a porter follows him with two more. Mother rushes to him and throws her arms around him while Daddy and I follow. Grandfather is stout with a fringe of gray hair on an almost bald head and a thick gray mustache and he has a gold watch on a chain across his vest that he used to let me hold so I could hear the ticking. He is dressed in a gray suit and I notice a black armband on one sleeve He gives me a kiss and his mustache tickles my cheek. I have not seen him since last Christmas, since before Uncle Edgar drowned, and he looks sad too and his face is not as round. He tells me how much I have grown and Mother says that I will be starting school next September at Potomac School. I can't decide whether I am happy about school or not.

Mother asks about Grandmother and Grandfather shakes his head. "I'm not sure that she'll ever be the same," he says. "Edgar was . . ." He does not finish his sentence and takes out a large white handkerchief and wipes his eyes quickly.

We get in the car and drive past the Lincoln Memorial. When I am bigger Daddy says he will take me to see it at night when it is all lit up. I am sitting in the front seat with Daddy who is driving and Mother is in back with Grandfather. I hear Grandfather say that Aunt Edith is off to Europe again and he mutters something about all her spending. I look out the window. The cherry blossoms are coming out and they look so pretty. Daddy turns up Massachusetts Avenue and we drive past all the embassies. Mother says the motion of the car is making her feel queasy.

"We're almost home," Daddy says and drives faster.

I turn around to look at Mother. She is pale and leaning on Grandfather who is patting her hand. I do not think I ever want to have a baby if it makes you feel sick all the time. Lavinia told me that the baby is in Mother's tummy and will come out when it is time. I don't understand how it got in there and she wouldn't tell me.

"Here we are," Daddy says, turning on to Tracy Place and pulling up in front of the house. Daffodils are blooming in the front yard but I am not allowed to pick them unless I ask permission. I did once and got spanked.

"I'm just going to lie down for a little bit," Mother says when we get in the house. "Why don't you show Grandfather your room and give him the picture you colored for him?"

"That was supposed to be a surprise," I say, hurt that Mother has given it away.

"That's all right," Grandfather says. "I want to see it. I hear you're very good at art."

I feel better and I hope he likes the picture. He follows me up the stairs to my room on the third floor and I hear him breathing heavily behind me. He is puffing and his face is red when we get to the top.

"Good exercise, those stairs," he says.

I love running up and down the stairs and I had never thought of it as exercise. We go in my room, the first one at the top of the landing. Lavinia has tidied it up so it looks neater than usual. I sleep in one bed and pile everything on the other bed. Now the only toy on the other bed is the doll that Uncle Edgar gave me. I point her out to Grandfather.

"That's the doll Uncle Edgar gave me when he was here. Her name is Mary. Isn't she pretty?"

Grandfather nods and looks away. He has to clear his throat before he is able to speak. "Let's see your picture," he says and I hand it to him. It is of a white kitten sitting in a field of flowers. The sky is blue with a big yellow sun.

"Very good," he says. "You have real artistic talent."

I am pleased that he likes it and I can tell he means it.

Sometimes grown-ups pretend and say "very nice" when they don't think so at all.

"Your grandmother wanted to be an artist. You must have inherited your talents from her. Yes, she could have had a real career. She was very good."

My grandmother an artist? I tried to imagine her in an artist's smock with paint on her hands working on a canvas but I couldn't. I could only see her dressed in gray trimmed with lace and a sad expression on her face. "Why didn't she become an artist?" I asked.

"Because she married me instead," Grandfather said. "And raised a family. A more suitable occupation for a lady."

"I'm going to be an artist when I grow up," I announced. "That's what I want to do."

"Fine." Grandfather patted me on the head. "Now let's go back downstairs and join your mother."

"You forgot your picture." I handed it to him.

"Oh, thank you. I'll get a frame for it and put it on my bureau."

Before he left I heard Mother tell Grandfather that she planned to name the new baby Edgar and he seemed pleased. Daddy didn't say anything. I'd rather have a baby sister. Sometimes I pretend that Mary is my sister and not just a doll and I make up conversations and we play together, but I know that it's just make-believe and Mary can't talk back to me. I'd like a real sister, one I could talk to and play games with. Lavinia says that the baby will be whatever God sends. How can God send a baby that's already in Mother's stomach and is making her sick? I wish someone would explain it to me.

3

MOTHER'S STOMACH IS GROWING bigger and she is knitting some white bootees for the baby. I listen to the click-click of her needles and stare at the photograph of Uncle Edgar in the silver frame on the piano. He is wearing his aviator's uniform from the war and he looks so handsome with the wings pinned to his chest. Now he has real ones in heaven, but I miss him and wish he could come to visit us.

"Mother, if Uncle Edgar is an angel, why can't he fly down here and see us?"

Mother looks startled. "I just dropped a stitch," she says, frowning and counting the loops on the needle.

There is something about the mention of Uncle Edgar's name that makes everybody change the subject and I wonder why they don't want to talk about him.

"How did he get up to heaven from the bottom of the ocean?"

"Barbara, if you don't mind, please let's not talk about it. My, it's hot this afternoon. Daddy should be home soon."

Every morning Lavinia closes all the windows and pulls down the blinds to keep the sun out but it doesn't help much.

On weekends we go out to the Chevy Chase Club and I want to learn how to swim but Mother and Daddy won't let me go in the pool because of something called polio that they say children catch in pools.

"Why don't you ask Lavinia to bring us some lemonade?" Mother asked.

"And some cookies?"

"Not too many. It will spoil your dinner."

I didn't care. Lavinia had made some lace cookies and I helped her mix the dough of butter and eggs and sugar and oatmeal and baking powder. I skipped happily out to the kitchen.

"Mother would like some lemonade and cookies," I said, reaching into the cookie jar and taking a lace cookie. It was thin and crumbly, pale yellow with a curly brown edge around it like lace and it broke in my fingers.

"Get your hand out of the cookie jar," Lavinia said. "I'll bring everything in to you on a tray."

I went back to the living room. Mother has stopped wearing black and I'm glad. She said it was too warm for the summer, but I think it depressed her, and Daddy too. She now wears gray or lavender. In August we are going to stay at the Greenbrier Hotel in White Sulphur Springs. Mother says it is in the mountains of West Virginia and it will be cool there. It is so hot in my room on the third floor that I am sleeping in the guest room on the second floor with the big four-poster bed, the room Grandfather stays in when he visits. And I have a fan going at night too. Lavinia is still in her hot room on the third floor and when I asked Mother why she didn't move her to the guest room she said it wasn't proper for servants. Daddy is talking about having rock wool put in the attic before next summer to make it cooler.

Mother has put down her knitting and is looking at the photograph of Uncle Edgar on the piano, but when she sees me she quickly turns away. But not before I see tears in her eyes.

"Lavinia is going to bring the lemonade and cookies," I tell her, hoping that will make her feel better.

She just nods absently, as if she is thinking of something else.

"Mother, how will the baby get out?"

She looks at me as if I am always asking questions she does not want to answer, but just then we hear the key turning in the lock and the front door opens. Daddy is home.

He comes over and kisses Mother and then me. He is perspiring and his seersucker jacket is sticking to him in the back.

"How was your day?" Mother asks.

He shrugs. "The same. The market went down ten points."

"We're just about to have some lemonade. Would you like some?"

"No thanks. I'll have something a little stronger."

Daddy goes out to the bar on the sunporch and pours himself a gin-and-tonic with lots of ice. Lavinia comes in with the lemonade and cookies. I take my glass and two cookies.

"Better use a napkin," Mother says. "Those cookies will crumble all over the sofa."

Wait till the baby comes, I think. Then there will be someone else to blame for spilling things. Lavinia says babies throw up all the time and do poo-poo in their pants. Mother is so fussy about the house I don't think she'll like that.

"What a rat race," says Daddy, taking a large sip of his drink.

I don't think Daddy likes going to work, but men have to. Women are supposed to stay home and take care of their children and make their husbands comfortable and happy. At least that's what Mother tells me. I said that Lavinia works for us and she said that was different.

"Black folks have to work," Lavinia told me. "Most times there ain't no man to support them."

Anything that Mother won't tell me I ask Lavinia and she explains it to me. Most of the time. Except about Uncle Edgar. There is some mystery about Uncle Edgar, but one day I will find out what it is.

4

THE HOUSE I GREW UP IN, the house on Tracy Place. Years later, now that both Mother and Daddy are dead, I stare at the framed picture of that house with the old-fashioned car parked in front, a black Packard with a running board because it was so high and a spare tire strapped on the side and large headlights like lamps. How different it is from the cars of today! The photograph must have been taken in the thirties. The house is white-washed brick, three stories, with a steep slate roof, and brick steps lead up to the front door. My room was in the rear overlooking the garden and the lily pond, so it doesn't show in the photograph. Annabel's room was across the hall. How strange to think of us in that house, and now. . . .

I would never have done to her what she did to me. But then, I am not Annabel.

We are back from White Sulphur Springs and I am getting ready for school next month. I have a new bookbag and new shoes and a lot of new skirts and blouses and sweaters. I also have a new friend whose family has bought the house next door. Her name is Sally and she has red hair and freckles. Her father is with the State Department and she says she is going to be in first grade at Potomac School in September too. I am glad and I hope they live there for a long time. Their kitchen door is right next to ours, so I can run out my kitchen and down the back steps and up a few more steps to Sally's back door. She has a little brother whose name is Jimmy. Sally says he is a pest. I tell her that I will have a baby brother or sister in November. Jimmy brought back a chameleon from Ringling Brothers Circus and put it on Sally's bed to scare her. I hope I have a sister and not a brother.

Mother is quite fat now and complains that her back hurts. I hear her talking on the telephone to a friend and she says she will be glad to get this all over with.

"If men had to go through this," she says, and stops when she sees me standing at her bedroom door. "Yes? What is it?" she asks, holding the phone away from her.

"Can I go play at Sally's?"

"Fine, but don't stay late. School starts tomorrow."

I run down the stairs and through the kitchen where Lavinia is peeling potatoes for dinner, and out the back door.

First day of school. I wonder if Sally is as nervous as I am? Lavinia wakes me up early and I get dressed in my new school outfit and brush my hair and go down to breakfast. Daddy is already up but Mother is still in bed. Daddy looks at me over the *Washington Post* and smiles.

"Well, the big day has arrived," he says. "My little Barbara is going off to school."

I don't know if I can eat anything, but Lavinia brings me orange juice and Wheatena and buttered toast. Daddy says he will drive me to school. I eat what I can and then go up to my bathroom and brush my teeth. I hope I'm not going to throw up. I wonder if they have a bathroom at school?

The Potomac School is on California Street and there is a big playground in back with a jungle-gym and a slide and swings. Daddy takes me to my classroom and I meet my teacher, Mrs. Neal. She is plump with gray hair and she leads me around the classroom and introduces me to the other children. Daddy leaves quickly and I am afraid I'm going to cry when I see him disappear down the hall and I want to run after him, but I bite my lip hard. Sally is not here yet but there are other girls and boys. Mrs. Neal shows me my desk. The top lifts up and I can put my bookbag inside. There are some yellow pencils and an eraser and some lined paper in the desk.

In front of the classroom is a large blackboard and chalk and on Mrs. Neal's desk is a globe of the world. I hear a fire engine go shrieking down Connecticut Avenue. Our classroom is on the second floor and I see a fire escape outside the window. I feel a pain in my stomach and I would like to be home playing with my dolls or building a log cabin with my Lincoln Logs. I will be glad when this first day of school is over.

Sally has arrived and she and her mother are talking to Mrs. Neal. I feel better when I see her and I hope she will be sitting near me, but Mrs. Neal gives her a desk on the other side of the classroom.

A bell rings and Mrs. Neal says we are to form an orderly line and go to assembly. I'm not sure what that is, but it turns out to be a gathering of the whole school in the gymnasium. A lady is playing the piano and we march in to music, a parade song I have heard before. The principal, Miss Skiffington, introduces herself and welcomes all the new pupils to Potomac School. Then we have a prayer and sing "America the Beautiful." After that we march back to our classroom. I try to catch Sally's eye but she is busy talking to the girl next to her. Mrs. Neal says there will be no talking, we are to march in silence. She looks strict and I haven't seen her smile yet except greeting the parents. Already I am afraid of her.

Another bell rings and the class begins. Mrs. Neal has each of us stand up and say our names. Then she asks us what our fathers do. Why does she want to know that? I say that my daddy goes to an office on Connecticut Avenue but I don't know exactly what he does there, something to do with stocks. Now that she has found out who we are, Mrs. Neal distributes notebooks. She writes our name on each one. Daddy has taught me some of the letters but I don't know all of them. Mrs. Neal has two extra notebooks and she puts them on her desk and says they are for two pupils whose fathers are in Congress so they won't be joining us until January when Congress resumes. She seems very impressed with what our fathers do. Aren't mothers important?

Mrs. Neal takes a piece of chalk and writes some letters on the blackboard. We are to copy them in our notebooks after her. Then she will call our names and we can write them on the blackboard. I watch her and try to copy the letters neatly in my notebook. I don't want her to be angry with me or think I am stupid.

Lavinia picks me up at noon and we walk home together. I can't wait to tell Mother all about my first day of school. Lavinia says she is still in bed and not feeling too well. I go to her room and open my bookbag and take out my notebook and the drawing I did in art class.

"Very good," Mother says, looking at my letters, but she doesn't seem all that interested. "Now go get your lunch."

"Aren't you going to get dressed?" I ask.

"A little later," Mother says. "Lavinia is going to bring me my lunch in bed."

Mother's room is so pretty with pale peach walls and lots of lacy pillows on her bed and a lace canopy above it. Daddy's room is next to it with a bathroom in between. Sally's mother and father sleep in the same bedroom in the same bed. I wonder why Mother and Daddy don't?

❄ ❄ ❄ ❄ ❄

In my dream, except that I do not know it is a dream until I wake up, Uncle Edgar and I are on a ship together. We are sailing close to an island that has palm trees and green mountains and white sandy beaches. Seagulls circle overhead as the ship moves through the water, rising and falling on the blue-green waves and a wave splashes on the deck and I feel frightened and I grab Uncle Edgar's hand, but he tells me not to be afraid, he will protect me. A seagull swoops down and picks up some food floating in the white foam trailing the ship. The ship turns and I see a large black freighter coming out of the harbor, it appears to be coming right toward us and I point it out to Uncle Edgar. Our ship gives three sharp blasts of its horn, but the freighter keeps coming, faster and faster, it is going to hit us I tell Uncle Edgar, but he says it will pass us, even though he looks worried and holds my hand tighter.

Now I cannot see the freighter anymore but suddenly there is a terrible sound of metal and wood splintering and the ship lurches and groans and sailors are shouting, words that are in a language I can't understand and a ship's officer runs past us yelling and waving his hands and I hear a woman shriek, "We've been hit! We're going to sink!" I look up at the lifeboats on the deck above, they are covered in canvas and look very small and I wonder how we're all going to fit in them and how they will lower them to the water.

We go around to the other side and we see the freighter has made a big hole in our ship and water is pouring in down where some of the cabins are and passengers are running around and no one knows what to do. Someone shouts something over the ship's intercom but no one can understand it. I am going to drown.

"I will take care of you," Uncle Edgar says.

The ship is going down fast, there is not enough time to lower the lifeboats. "We'll have to jump and swim for it," a man says. "Watch out for the propellers." "And sharks," another says.

I do not want to die. Uncle Edgar grabs a life preserver and straps me in it. He does not take one for himself and I ask him why. "Women and children first," he says. Uncle Edgar is going to drown. No, no! He throws me in the water. I swallow salt water mixed with oil and I think I am going to choke. I come to the surface and start coughing and sputtering, trying to spit out the horrible taste and thrashing my arms around in the water and kicking my feet. Uncle Edgar is still on the deck helping ladies and children into life preservers. There won't be enough left for him. "Uncle Edgar! Uncle Edgar!"

I am sobbing and Mother and Daddy are beside me and I am in my own bed and I have knocked over the glass of water on the night table next to my bed and the sheets and blanket are all wet.

5

HERE IS A PHOTOGRAPH of Mother in a sleigh drawn by a black horse with a white forehead and muzzle. She is all bundled up in a coat with a fur collar and her hands are hidden in a fur muff and a fur robe covers the rest of her. She wears a large hat that looks like it has feathers on top and beside her sits the coachman dressed in a dark uniform with brass buttons and a cap that resembles the helmet of a London bobby. The street is packed with heavy snow but the sidewalk has mostly been cleared. They are outside a church because you can see the stained glass windows. Mother is looking at the camera, the coachman straight ahead at the horse as he holds the reins stiffly in his hands. Are they waiting for someone? The sleigh won't hold more than two persons. It is in Pittsburgh on a cold winter's day, or it could even be early spring because it often snows there around Easter.

I wish someone had marked all these photographs instead of just tossing them in a trunk. It is so hard to figure out some of them or who the people are.

Mother has fixed up a nursery all in blue for Baby Edgar. But what if he's a girl?

The crib is blue with white lambs painted on it and there is a matching chifforobe and an armchair covered in blue-and-white plaid. The walls are pale blue with figures of Humpty Dumpty sitting on a wall and Winken, Blinken and Nod and other nursery rhyme characters. Mother had an artist friend paint them. I asked if I could help, but Mother said no. She let me watch though and I told Mother's friend that I was going to be an artist when I grew up. She just smiled and didn't say anything. I was going to show her some of my drawings but then I decided not to.

Later I heard Daddy tell Mother that it was nice of her to help out the friend who didn't have a husband and needed the money.

The nursery reeks of wet paint and I can smell it in my room right across the hall, but Mother says the odor will be gone by the time Baby Edgar arrives. I hope so, because it makes me want to throw up.

Today is my sixth birthday. Mother says I was supposed to be a Halloween baby but I was born two weeks early. I think it would be fun to have a Halloween birthday and then everyone could wear costumes to my party. Anyway, after school Sally and some of my friends are coming over to play games and Daddy has rented some cartoons to show on his movie projector. He is coming home early from his brokerage office. Then we will have ice cream and birthday cake and open the presents.

I know what my wish is going to be when I blow out the candles on my cake. A baby sister.

Would I have wished so hard for a sister if I had known the tragedy she would bring? But we cannot look into the future, and perhaps it is just as well.

The leaves have all turned to red and orange and gold and I colored a tree with autumn colors for art class and I got an A. Only two more days till Halloween. I can hardly wait! Marian Wilson is having a Halloween party at her house and we are going to go trick or treating. I have a witch costume and a wig of long gray hair and one of my front teeth came out so I won't have to black it with a crayon the way Lavinia suggested to look like a witch.

Mother and Daddy are very upset about something. They are talking about a terrible crash and I asked Lavinia if it was a car crash and she said no, it was the stock market that had crashed. I don't understand. How could a stock market crash?

Daddy is in the library reading an article from the newspaper to Mother. He appears in a state of shock. "I can't believe he jumped," he said. "I went to Yale with him."

"Who jumped?" I ask.

Daddy suddenly notices that I have come in the room and puts down the newspaper. "An old friend of mine," he says.

"Where did he jump from?"

"He had an accident," Mother says quickly. "He was sitting on a window ledge and he fell."

"Then why did Daddy say he jumped?"

"Please, Barbara, let's not talk about it anymore," Mother says, and then Lavinia comes in and announces that dinner is ready and we all go in the dining room.

The Halloween party has been cancelled. Marian Wilson was not in school today and Mrs. Neal told the class that her father had died suddenly. At recess Sally whispered to me that Mr. Wilson had committed suicide. I wasn't sure what that meant and she said he had killed himself, she had overheard her parents talking about it, and then I thought of Daddy's friend from Yale who had fallen out a window but Daddy told Mother he jumped when he didn't know I was in the room, and then I wondered about the mysterious drowning of Uncle Edgar. Did he commit suicide? Is that why no one wanted to talk about it when I asked?

Anyway, we are to wear our Halloween costumes to school tomorrow and have apple cider and cookies as a special treat. Lavinia helped me carve a pumpkin to put in the window, a big smiling jack-o'-lantern with eyes and a nose and three teeth. She has baked two pumpkin pies and Daddy says he will take Sally and me trick or treating around the neighborhood, so I get to wear my Halloween costume after all, but I am sorry about Marian's father.

Lavinia won't tell me anything, so I have decided to ask Mother about Uncle Edgar. I keep thinking about it, especially at night when I am trying to get to sleep and I see him floating on the ocean and then sinking down into its murky deep green depths tangled with seaweed and fish swimming by his face and bubbles coming out of his mouth.

Lavinia says he is at peace now, poor man. Leave him rest in peace, child. But I can't. I must know the truth.

Wouldn't bring him back, Lavinia says. But I don't care. I want to know. I just have to find the right time to ask her.

Mother is lying on her chaise longue looking out the window at a squirrel running across the branch of an oak tree. Her stomach bulges like a balloon that has been blown up and I wonder if it hurts to have it stretch so. I'm sure she will be happy when the baby comes out.

On her dressing table there is a photograph of Uncle Edgar right behind all her perfume bottles. He is wearing a dark suit and tie and his arms are crossed across his chest. His white shirt has a round collar and there is a stickpin in his tie and his shirt has fancy cufflinks. He looks much younger than in the photograph on the piano in his flier's uniform and Mother told me that was taken when he was in college at Amherst.

Mother sees me and smiles. "Look at the cute squirrel. We'll have to get some peanuts for him."

"Yes," I say, but there is something else on my mind. "Mother, I want to ask you something."

"You look very serious. It must be something important."

"It is. It's about Uncle Edgar."

Her face clouds over, the way it always does at the mention of Uncle Edgar, but I am going to find out once and for all what really happened.

"Did he kill himself like Marian Wilson's father and Daddy's friend from Yale?"

Mother takes a quick intake of breath and one hand goes to her throat. She looks too stricken to say anything and I wonder if I should have just left the subject alone, but then she pats a place on the chaise longue beside her and says, "Sit down, Barbara."

I sit down, though there isn't much room with her big stomach. She starts to talk, looking off into the distance and stroking my hair. "It's a very sad story," she says. "Because it was an accident. One of those freak accidents that sometimes happen." She pauses. "The cabin on the ship had been freshly painted and the smell was so strong that Uncle Edgar opened the porthole to get some fresh air. And he fell out."

Something about the story didn't sound right, but weren't grown-ups supposed to tell the truth? I remembered Mother saying to Daddy, "But why did he do it? Why?" Did she mean why did Uncle Edgar open the porthole? No, that wasn't what she meant.

"I see," I said, but I didn't. There was a thick book on the table beside the chaise longue with a bookmark in it where she had stopped. The cover had an angel on it and I could read some of the title.

Mother noticed me looking at it. "It's called *Look Homeward, Angel*," she said. "It's a novel by a new writer, Thomas Wolfe."

"Is it good?"

"Yes, it's very interesting."

"It would take me a long time to read a book that long," I said.

"That's why you go to school. To learn how. Do you know that there are some people in this country who can't read or write? Poor people who live in the mountains of Kentucky and Tennessee. Can you imagine what it would be like to be a grown-up and not be able to read or to write your name? All they can do is make an X on a piece of paper when they have to sign something. So you see how important it is to get an education."

"I can write my name now. Do you want me to show you?"

"Not right now," Mother said. "Why don't you go outside and play? Ask Lavinia to give you some peanuts to feed the squirrel."

6

ANOTHER PHOTOGRAPH of Mother, this one marked for a change. On the back is written: Myra, Lake Chautauqua, N.Y. August 1909, so she must have been nineteen. It was taken on the porch of the Athenaeum Hotel and she is sitting in a wicker chair wearing a Gibson girl suit with leg of mutton sleeves and a white ruffled blouse with a cameo brooch at her throat. Her hair is puffed up on top of her head and she wears simple pearl button earrings and a gold bracelet, her hands resting in her lap. But the most extraordinary thing about the photograph is her hat. It is huge and over-powering with a dozen stuffed white doves roosting on it. Her expression resembles that of the Mona Lisa the first time I saw it in the Louvre, mysterious and knowing.

As I study the photograph, I can't help thinking what a fit today's animal rights groups would have if they could see that hat!

Mother told me that they spent many summers at Lake Chautauqua to get away from the heat of Pittsburgh and also so that Grandmother could enjoy the arts festival. Grandfather seldom joined her except for an occasional weekend, since he was so busy with business, but Grandmother was able to immerse herself in music and art.

No one else in our family is artistic except me, so I guess I do inherit my talent from her.

Everyone says Mrs. Neal is a good teacher, but I think she is mean. Today she took a page I had written and held it up before the class. "Very good, Barbara," she said. I was pleased because I had tried to make my alphabet letters the way she wanted and I started to smile and then she added, "But not good enough," and ripped the paper in half. Michael Moriarty laughed and I bit my lip hard so I couldn't cry. I'm glad my art teacher Miss Dillard doesn't tear up my drawings. I really like her and she has chosen me to do the Thanksgiving poster for the first grade.

We are making Pilgrim costumes for Thanksgiving. The girls have long gray dresses with big white collars and white caps and the boys black suits with white collars and stiff hats with brims made of cardboard. We are copying the costumes from pictures of Pilgrims in a book. We will wear them to assembly the Wednesday before Thanksgiving and we each have to bring some food from home to distribute to the poor.

It must be awful to be poor and not have enough to eat and have people bring you charity baskets. Mrs. Neal says that none of us realize how fortunate we are.

I hope that I will have something special to be thankful for by Thanksgiving and every night before going to bed I look out my window and pick out an especially bright star and say, "Star light, star bright, give me the wish I wish tonight. Please, please, send me a baby sister."

Mother has gone to the hospital. She started to have bad pains right after dinner and they were getting closer and closer together, so Daddy drove her there. Lavinia said that sometimes babies take a long time to come, when I told her I was going to stay up all night. And besides, she reminded me, there is school tomorrow.

I don't care. I am going to keep pinching myself so I don't fall asleep.

It is morning. My alarm clock just went off and woke me up, so I guess I must have fallen asleep after all. I jump out of bed and run down to Daddy's room but he is not there, so I go down the back stairs to the kitchen and call Lavinia.

"Child, what are you doing in your bare feet? And with no robe either. You'll catch your death of cold."

"Lavinia, has the baby been born yet? Have you heard from Daddy?"

"No. Like I told you, sometimes babies take a long time. Now go get dressed."

Just then the telephone rings and I start to run for it.

"I'll get it," Lavinia says. She picks up the phone and a broad grin spreads over her face. "I'm so glad. And the missus came through it all right?"

"It's Daddy! Let me talk to him."

"Here's Miss Barbara," Lavinia says and hands me the receiver.

"You have a little sister," Daddy says. "She weighs six pounds, eight ounces. And Mother is fine and sends her love."

A sister. My wish came true! Goodbye, Baby Edgar. I knew you were a girl after all. "When can I see the baby?"

"When Mother brings her home."

"When will that be?"

"In about five days. Now you be good and mind Lavinia and I'll be home in a little while."

A sister! I can hardly contain my joy. I dance around the kitchen singing at the same time.

"You go get dressed right now," Lavinia says. "Or you'll end up in the hospital with pneumonia."

"Then I'll be able to see my sister."

"Oh, no. You'd be in a different part of the hospital. They don't let nobody with infections near those new babies."

"I wonder what they'll name her?" For months she has been called Baby Edgar and her room and everything in it is blue.

"I expect they'll think of something," Lavinia says. "Now you get dressed and have your breakfast and Bates will drive you to school."

Bates is our new chauffeur. He sleeps in the cellar in a room next to the laundry and opposite the furnace room. His room is dark with only one tiny window. It is very gloomy and I wouldn't want to sleep there.

I go back up to my room and get dressed for school.

"Good morning, Bates."

"Good morning, Miss Barbara," Bates says, opening the car door for me.

"Did you know that I have a baby sister?"

"Yes, Lavinia told me the good news."

I get in and throw my bookbag on the car seat beside me and Bates gets in the front. Bates is old and has a lined face and gray hair. He is so nice. Daddy says he used to drive for one of the embassies. I wonder if he has children? Mother says it is rude to ask people personal questions about their lives, but I would like to know. Anyway it's hard to talk because there is a glass partition between the chauffeur's seat and the back of the car. I look out the window and watch Mr. Owens, who lives on the corner, walking his collie along Tracy Place. It only takes about five minutes to drive to school. I can hardly wait to tell everyone my news!

I am in bed with a cold and Mother is coming home tomorrow with Annabel. Yes, that is what they have named her. Lavinia says I have to be all over my cold before I go near the baby or I might give it to her. I am lying here smelling of Vicks Vaporub that Lavinia rubbed on my chest and put a flannel cloth over that and I am looking at the bare tulip trees outside my windows and feeling very sorry for myself. I am wheezing and coughing and I have a fever. It's not fair that I have to be sick now!

They are home. I hear them go by my closed door and into Baby Edgar's room—I mean Annabel's—across the hall. I hope she likes the color blue, but I guess they can always repaint it. Mother is in her bedroom on the second floor and the trained nurse who came home with them from the hospital will bring Annabel down to Mother's room for her feedings. Daddy comes in to see me and ask how I am feeling and says he hopes I will be better soon so I can see my baby sister. I can't see Mother either because she might catch my cold. I feel like a prisoner in this room all by myself with Lavinia bringing my meals to me on a tray.

"Don't want to say 'I told you so,'" Lavinia says as she brings me chicken noodle soup with saltines and Jell-O. "That's what you get for running around on cold floors in bare feet."

I feel bad enough already without her saying that.

"I'm not hungry."

"Oh, no, you don't pull that on me." Lavinia puts the tray on my bed. "You've got to eat to get well. Feed a cold, starve a fever."

"What if I have both?"

Lavinia doesn't have an answer to that one, so I sit up and slowly sip my soup while she sits in a chair watching me.

It is Thanksgiving and I am still sick in bed, so I missed wearing my Pilgrim costume at school and Lavinia had to bring me my turkey dinner on a tray. The doctor came to see me and listened to my chest with a stethoscope and heard me cough and said I had bronchitis. He also left some horrible-tasting medicine for me.

Annabel is two weeks old and I still haven't seen her.

Annabel cries a lot, especially at night, and she keeps me awake. I wonder if all babies cry that much? I can hear her screaming in her room across the hall. Mrs. Meier, the trained nurse who came home from the hospital with Mother and Annabel, sleeps on a cot in Annabel's room. I guess she's not getting much sleep either, but Lavinia says that's what she's being paid for. "Those trained nurses get plenty of money," Lavinia told me. I don't think she likes someone else being in the house, especially another person she has to cook for and who is getting paid more than she is.

I wonder if I cried that much when I was a baby?

Finally I am over my bronchitis and no longer contagious so I can see Annabel. I go into the nursery with Mother and Annabel is asleep in her crib but Mrs. Meier says it is almost time for her to wake up. She looks so tiny and she doesn't have much hair. I can't see what color her eyes are but as I peer through the slats of the crib she opens her eyes and smiles. At least I think it's a smile, but then her face gets red and she starts to cry.

"It's time to feed her," Mrs. Meier says.

Mother sits down in the chair and Mrs. Meier hands Annabel to her. Mother unbuttons her blouse and Annabel sucks greedily. I look around her room. She has so many toys. I wind up a musical giraffe and bring it over so she can see it. The giraffe turns its neck around in a circle as the music plays.

"Don't do that, Barbara," Mother says. "It will disturb her while she's eating."

I wonder when Annabel will be big enough for me to play with her? She is smaller than my doll Mary that Uncle Edgar gave me, but I guess she'll grow. I put the giraffe back on the shelf. Christmas is coming in three weeks. Michael Moriarty told me there isn't a Santa Claus, it's your parents who bring the presents, but I don't believe him. I hope we have snow for Christmas so I can build a snowman and show it to Annabel.

Daddy told me we are getting a new nursemaid next week because we don't need a trained nurse anymore for Annabel. Mrs. Meier was just supposed to come home with Mother and Annabel from the hospital and stay a few weeks.

"Mrs. Meier only takes care of new babies," Daddy said. "And besides, she's too expensive."

Kristin is the new nursemaid who has come to take care of Annabel. She is Swedish and speaks with a sing-song lilt. She has blonde hair and blue eyes and a dimple when she smiles and I think she is very pretty. Daddy thinks so too. He spends a lot more time in the nursery than he did when Mrs. Meier was here.

Kristin noticed the photograph of Uncle Edgar on the piano in his aviator's uniform.

"Who's the handsome man?" she asked.

"My Uncle Edgar," I said. "He's dead."

"What a pity. And so young."

"He drowned at sea." She looked interested so I continued. "He was on a ship and they had just painted his cabin and he leaned out his porthole to get some air and he fell out."

"How is that possible? To fall out a porthole?"

"But he did. That's what Mother told me."

Kristin studied the photograph. "How sad."

"But now he's an angel in heaven with wings and a halo and we'll see him when we go through the Pearly Gates."

"What nonsense is that?" Kristin said.

"Don't you believe in heaven?"

"I don't know what there is beyond. But I intend to have a good time in this life." She smiled, showing the dimple in one cheek and just then Mother came into the room.

Daddy says he is going to get a tiny tree for the nursery and put miniature lights and ornaments on it for Annabel. He says he made one for me when I was a baby and I can help him with this one for Annabel and put on the ornaments.

Kristin told me about how in Sweden on December thirteenth they have something called a "Festival of Lights," and the eldest daughter in a family is chosen to be Saint Lucia and bring the breakfast tray to her parents with coffee, sweet saffron buns and ginger cookies, singing "Santa Lucia" and wearing a long white dress with a red sash and a crown made of a green wreath with lighted candles.

"Don't the candles make her hair catch on fire?" I ask.

"Not if one is careful."

She has promised to dress me up as Saint Lucia and show me.

Christmas Eve. I am lying in bed trying to get to sleep but I keep thinking about tomorrow and what Santa Claus will bring me. I hope I get a dollhouse. I left a note for Santa Claus by the fireplace in the living room so he can see it as soon as he comes down the chimney and a glass of milk and two brownies in case he is hungry.

I made the mistake of telling Mother about Saint Lucia and the wreath of lighted candles and Mother said it was far too dangerous and could set the house on fire and forbade Kristin and me to do it. I have learned my lesson and I won't tell her anything in future but will just go ahead without saying anything. Kristin's family sent her a tin of Swedish ginger cookies in shapes of stars, reindeer, and Christmas trees, and she invited Lavinia and me to share them with her after Mother and Daddy left for Christmas Eve carol services at St. Thomas Episcopal Church. So I got to stay up real late. Kristin brought Annabel downstairs to show her the tree but she just blinked her eyes at it and started to cry. Then Kristin rocked her and sang her a Swedish lullaby. Kristin has a pretty voice and Annabel stopped crying. It will be more fun next year when Annabel is bigger and can play with me.

My room is cold and my feet are freezing, even under two blankets. I wonder if it's going to snow? Then I can build a snowman after I open all my presents. I love Christmas! Grown-ups don't seem to like it as much. I wonder why?

Suddenly my eyelids feel heavy and I can't keep my eyes open any longer. Please, Santa, bring me a dollhouse.

"Merry Christmas!"

It is Daddy standing by my bed smiling and holding out my robe and slippers. "Let's go downstairs and see what Santa Claus has brought."

My radiator is making hissing sounds and I quickly put on my bathrobe and slippers and run ahead of him down the stairs and fling open the living room doors. There next to the tree is the most beautiful dollhouse.

"Look, Daddy, Santa brought me a dollhouse!"

Just then Mother comes in carrying Annabel. She looks at Daddy and they seem pleased that I am so happy about the dollhouse.

Daddy points to the coffee table where I left the note. "Santa Claus drank the milk and ate the brownies," he says, but I am busy examining my dollhouse. It has a living room with a grand piano and a sofa and chairs and a hooked rug and paintings on the wall just like our living room, and the dining room has plates of food and a tiny silver tea set and a maid in a uniform but she is white and not black like Lavinia, and there is a kitchen with a stove and icebox and sink and a cupboard with little bags of flour and a ham on a platter. The hallway has a grandfather clock and upstairs are two bedrooms and a bathroom. One bedroom has a canopy bed and the other bedroom has twin beds. There is a mother and a father doll and a girl and boy, and on the third floor is a nursery with a baby in a crib.

"Just like Annabel," I exclaim.

"These are real electric lights," Daddy says and plugs the light cord into the socket and the dollhouse lights up.

"And real shades in the windows," Mother adds.

"Santa Claus was pretty good to you," says Daddy.

There are other presents gaily wrapped but I am too excited about my dollhouse to stop playing with it. Annabel has a white teddy bear and a musical carousel and a lamb with a bell round its neck, but I have the best present of all.

Lavinia comes in to wish us Merry Christmas and to say that breakfast is ready, but I don't want to tear myself away from my dollhouse. It is the best Christmas ever!

Years later I still think of that dollhouse. When Annabel had daughters and I had a son, Mother gave the dollhouse to her and her girls destroyed it. I wanted to keep it but I was living in Europe then and Annabel lived nearby. But what I resent is that Mother never even asked me if it was all right before she gave my dollhouse to Annabel. After my nieces wrecked it they gave it to some charity and I never saw it again.

But it remains in my memory as the most beautiful dollhouse and the best Christmas of my childhood. The following year I found out that what Michael Moriarty had told me was true, there is no Santa Claus and it is your parents who buy the presents.

After that, Christmas was never the same.

7

KRISTIN IS LEAVING. When I came home from school she was already packing her clothes and she told me that Mother had fired her. I don't know why. Mother says she will take care of Annabel herself until the agency finds someone else.

Things are very tense between Mother and Daddy and I wonder if it is because of Kristin. After dinner I was passing Daddy's room and Mother was in there talking to him.

"How could you, Lamont? And with a servant in our own home?" I heard Mother say.

"Your imagination is working overtime, Myra. Nothing happened."

"I don't believe you." A door slams shut and Mother goes into her own room.

I start to run up the stairs but just then Daddy comes out and sees me. He looks at me without saying anything and goes downstairs. I go up to my room and rearrange the furniture in my dollhouse until it is time for bed. I hear Mother go into Annabel's room and then she comes by to see me.

"Time to get your bath, Barbara." She looks as if she has been crying.

"Yes, Mother." I want to ask her about Kristin but it doesn't seem like a good idea. Just before dinner a cab came and Kristin left in it. I didn't even get to say goodbye to her. I liked her and I'm sorry I wasn't able to be Saint Lucia and wear a wreath of lighted candles in my hair.

Another photograph from the trunk of Mother, Annabel, and me. It is taken in the garden in spring and Mother is sitting in a wicker chair next to a white lilac bush holding Annabel on her lap and I am standing beside her with a sprig of lilac in my hand looking not at them but at the camera with a pensive expression. Mother is smiling happily and wearing a black dress with a large white lace collar without her usual pearls. Perhaps she is afraid Annabel will pull on them and break them? But that is later when Annabel will clean out Mother's safe deposit box before I get there and take the pearls and almost all of her jewelry, along with her tax-free bonds.

But here we look so young and innocent in happier days. Mother so pretty with her short wavy hair that she never had to curl, me with my straight hair, and Annabel with golden ringlets.

A moment frozen in time.

We have a new nursemaid for Annabel. Her name is Tillie and she is from West Virginia. Tillie isn't pretty like Kristin, in fact she is quite homely with stringy mouse-colored hair and heavy legs and large red hands, but she seems very nice. I guess I will get used to her, though I miss Kristin and I'm sorry she had to leave. When I asked Lavinia why she said, "Better you don't ask." And then she muttered something under her breath about Swedish girls being "free and easy."

I know Mother likes Tillie better than Kristin, and Annabel is probably too little to tell the difference.

Grandfather and Grandmother are coming to visit us on their way to Pinehurst, North Carolina. Mother says they are going to stay at the Carolina Hotel for two months while they look for a house to buy there to spend the winter months. Pittsburgh gets too cold and Grandmother has had pneumonia twice, so the doctor told her she must go somewhere warmer.

"How long will they be here?" I ask.

"Only two days. They've never seen Annabel and they want to see her."

And not me? I feel hurt, but then Mother adds, "We'll go to meet their train at Union Station and you can come with us."

"Is Annabel coming too?"

"No, she'll stay at the house with Tillie."

I feel better. I haven't seen Grandmother for quite a long while, since before Uncle Edgar was drowned.

"When are Daddy's parents coming to see us?" We have gone to visit them in Charleston but they have never come to Washington. Perhaps it's because Grandmother Ashford is an invalid and it is hard for her to travel in her wheelchair.

Mother purses her lips. "At another time," she says.

"Well, how's my Barbara?" Grandfather says, giving me a big hug. He smells of cigar smoke and bay rum.

Grandmother looks very pale and much older than when I last saw her. Is it because of Uncle Edgar? Her skin feels like the papery Chinese flowers we have in a tall vase in the library that I am afraid will crumble when I touch them. Her clothes have a scent of lavender and I admire the brooch she has pinned at her throat on her ruffled blouse, a lilac-colored stone surrounded by tiny pearls.

"It's an amethyst." Grandmother fingers it and I notice the raised blue veins on her hand. "If you like it, I'll leave it to you in my will."

That isn't why I mentioned it because I don't want her to die and I think a person has to die before you get something in a will, like Uncle Edgar, but I haven't gotten what he left me yet. Then Grandfather starts talking about Aunt Edith and all her spending. Mother glances at the glass partition but it is closed tight and Bates can't hear what we are saying and besides he is busy driving the car.

"Edith is sending Jean to an expensive boarding school in Switzerland and she expects me to pay for it," he says. "I told her there were plenty of good schools in this country, but she insisted that Jean could only get a proper education at this place in Lausanne."

"They speak French all the time," says Grandmother.

"In the meantime Edith is going to toot all over Europe spending more of my money." Grandfather scowls. "She's already gone through what Randolph left her."

"Maybe she'll get married again," Mother says.

"She'd better marry a banker," says Grandfather.

"When we have our new house in Pinehurst you'll have to come and visit us," Grandmother says, attempting to change the subject. "It's so pretty there with pine trees and holly and several golf courses. Your grandfather will be able to play golf every day."

But Grandfather is not about to be diverted. He goes on complaining about Aunt Edith until Bates pulls up in front of our house on Tracy Place.

Annabel is just waking up from her nap.

"What a pretty baby," Grandfather says.

Grandmother holds her and rocks her. "They grow up so fast," she says. "All of a sudden they're gone and out of your life." I see tears in her eyes. Is she thinking of Uncle Edgar? Mother told me she had two older sisters she never knew because they died as babies. They were born after Aunt Edith, so that's why there is such an age difference between Mother and Aunt Edith. They are angels in heaven too with wings like Uncle Edgar and flying through the sky playing harps.

Annabel starts to cry and Mother says, "I think she needs

changing." Suddenly there is an awful smell. Annabel has done pooh-pooh in her diaper. Tillie steps over and takes Annabel from Grandmother and we leave the nursery. Annabel is still screaming as we go down the stairs.

I have the amethyst brooch now. Grandmother left it to me I her will the way she said she would and I wear it on a violet tweed suit and think of her, the woman who wanted to be an artist and wasn't, who loved colors and beauty and whose life was filled with tragedy.

In retrospect I see it all so clearly, the events I could not evaluate when I was living in their midst. Serena my grandmother, Myra my mother, Annabel my sister.

At night when I cannot sleep they emerge like characters in a play and speak their parts and vanish into the past again, the family album closes. Not much time remains so I must get it all down the way it was. Could we have changed it? Or was it all written in the stars and we played our roles and then disappeared, leaving frosty fingerprints on the windowpane of life.

8

I CRIED WHEN I SAID GOODBYE to the house in Pinehurst for the last time. The dogwood was in full bloom with pink and white blossoms and it had never looked more beautiful. The plump real estate lady was happily snapping pictures to show to prospective clients, telling Annabel and me that now Pinehurst is more of a year-round place to live than it was when Grandfather bought it and she was sure she could sell it soon. It hurt to think of strangers living there and I said hopefully, "Perhaps a nice doctor and his family who would love it the way my parents and grandparents did," while the real estate lady was marking on a list: No air-conditioning, three antiquated baths, kitchen needs remodeling. In other words, a charming wreck in a prime location, nearly two acres opposite the Carolina Hotel which is now called the Pinehurst Hotel and surrounded by modern condominiums. Annabel is less sentimental than I am, all that interests her is the price we will get for the house. "Whoever buys it will probably gut it," she told me.

I took a final walk down the long winding driveway bordered by pines and deodars and watched two squirrels scamper across a branch. At the entrance was a sign: ASHFORD, with a red cardinal on it, the sign Daddy had made a few years before he died because people had difficulty finding the house and often drove past it. I picked up a pinecone to pack in my suitcase. So many memories. . . .

Christmas in Pinehurst. Annabel is three and I am nine. I love Grandfather's house in Pinehurst, a rambling wooden two-story painted white with green shutters. It is informal and cheerful, unlike their house in Pittsburgh, with lots of places to play hide-and-seek. I especially like the dining room with the round table of olive green decorated with pink roses and matching chairs. Grandmother said it came from Austria. Above the buffet is a beautiful painting of wisteria and iris in a gold vase. The wisteria has trailing purple blossoms like the wisteria vine that grows outside Grandfather's bedroom window.

Annabel got a tricycle for Christmas and I can see her out the windows of the sunporch where I am curled up in front of a fire reading *Heidi*. She has on a blue snowsuit and matching bonnet and Mother and Grandmother are with her. Grandfather has taken Daddy to play golf at the Pinehurst Country Club. I promised Mother and Daddy that I wouldn't tell Anabel there isn't any Santa Claus until she finds out for herself and I have kept my promise. I wish I still believed in him though, because Christmas isn't as much fun when you know your parents buy the presents.

I got a diary for Christmas. It is green leather with my name printed on it in gold and a little gold key. I am going to write something in it every day.

Suddenly there is a scream from the driveway and I can't see anything from here but I can hear Annabel crying. I throw down my book and run to the front door and fling it open.

Annabel has fallen off her tricycle and is lying in the driveway and her nose is all bloody and blood is running down and staining her blue snowsuit.

"Get some towels," Mother says. She has a handkerchief pressed to Annabel's nose to try to stop the blood but it is seeping right through. "And tell Hilda to call the doctor."

Hilda is Grandmother's cook. Tillie has gone to visit her family in West Virginia for the holidays and will join us when we return to Washington next week. I rush toward the kitchen and almost collide in the pantry with Hilda who is coming to see what has happened.

"Annabel fell off her tricycle." I am so frightened I can hardly get the words out. Nothing must happen to Annabel! "We need towels and Mother says to call the doctor."

Hilda hands me some clean dishtowels and I run outside with them. Annabel is sitting up, still crying, and Mother grabs a towel and wipes the blood off her face.

"I think she's mostly scared," Grandmother says.

"Does anything hurt, baby?" Mother asked. "Bad tricycle. We'll put it away."

"No!" yells Annabel, "I want it!" She gets to her feet and I can see a scrape on her forehead and her nose is still bleeding.

Hilda comes back. "I've phoned Doctor Brady and he's on his way from Southern Pines," she says.

"And call Mr. Ashford at the Pinehurst Country Club," Mother says. "He's on the golf course with Mr. Calhoun. Have them paged."

"Yes, ma'am."

"Let's go inside, Myra," Grandmother says. She puts her arm around Annabel. "You're going to be fine. We'll just wash your face."

"She could have a concussion," Mother says, moving the tricycle out of the driveway and onto the lawn.

"Daddy isn't going to take my tricycle away, is he?" Annabel asks. "I can ride it. I'm not too little."

"Of course you can," Grandmother said. "It just takes practice. Like everything else. Let's go inside and sit in front of the fire and I'll tell you about the time I fell from a horse. We were riding along the bridle path and the horse stumbled and I went sailing right over his head."

"And then what happened?" Annabel asked. "Did you get hurt?"

"I landed on the pine needles and I got a few bruises, but mostly it was my pride that was hurt because I wasn't able to stay on the horse. But the next day I got up and rode him again and everything was fine. And you will be too."

"I'll help you learn to ride your tricycle, Annabel," I offered, glad that she was walking and appeared to be all right.

Mother threw me a grateful look. "That would be nice of you, Barbara. Aren't you lucky to have a big sister, Annabel?"

"I want to ride my tricycle now," Annabel said. "I don't want to see the doctor. I don't like doctors. They hurt you."

"But Doctor Brady is so nice," Grandmother said.

"And he'll just check you over to see that you didn't break anything when you fell," said Mother.

Annabel pouted.

"Let's sit in by the fire," Grandmother said, "and Hilda can bring us some hot chocolate to drink."

Outside of a nosebleed and a few scratches, it turned out that Annabel hadn't seriously hurt herself, and the next day she was back on her tricycle with me helping her. It wouldn't be the last time I would pick her up after a fall and help her get her life together.

Like many good intentions, I didn't write in my diary every day. I found it recently stored in a drawer and looked through it. Some of the people mentioned in it I had trouble remembering, but there is one entry from May 1933 that, in view of what my cousin Jean did later, I found interesting.

"My cousin Jean is going to be presented at the Court of St. James and she has to wear a long white dress and gloves and a headband with plumes and learn to curtsey and walk backward because you can never turn your back on royalty. Daddy told Mother that Aunt Edith thinks no man is good enough for Jean except the Prince of Wales. Aunt Jean is very tall and in the photographs I have seen of the Prince of Wales he looks short. All the ladies are trying to marry the Prince of Wales. I don't think he looks very handsome. Anyway, Aunt Edith is beside herself with joy that Jean has been accepted to be presented and they are leaving for London in two weeks, with a visit to Paris afterward. It sounds exciting and I hope I can go to those places some day.

Here is my graduation picture from Potomac School, all of us in short white dresses carrying sheaths of daisies and snapdragons. There are no boys in this photograph of the eighth grade because after the fourth grade the boys went on to Saint Albans or somewhere else. I am fourteen and wearing a pale Tangee lipstick and my hair is curled. Mother took me to her beauty parlor and had them give me a permanent to do something about my "impossible straight hair." I still had to put it up in curlers at night, in spite of the permanent, and when it rained it got all frizzy.

Here we all are before we go off on our separate ways to different boarding schools and lives that will take diverse paths, and some of us will never meet again. There is Sally with her red hair and freckles and big grin, and Fabienne, the daughter of the French Ambassador who became my friend. I wanted to change my name to something more exotic instead of just plain Barbara. Funny, but staring at the photograph I can't remember that graduation day at all. Maybe it is because I was so terrified that I might not pass eighth grade and therefore not graduate as my grades weren't all that good, mostly B's and C's, except for art and French in which I got A's. I recall waiting for my final grades and looking with apprehension at the report card, then seeing with relief that I had passed and would graduate with the others. If I hadn't, I think I would have killed myself from the humiliation. But the day itself is a blank. Mother and Daddy must have been there and Annabel. And I have my diploma with its fancy scroll and gold seal to prove it.

The thing I do remember clearly is that the winter after my graduation from Potomac, Grandmother died. I was at Miss Porter's in Farmington, Connecticut, a school I had chosen because I didn't have to take geometry or science, unlike Miss Madeira's, where many of my Potomac classmates went, but could instead major in languages, art, and archery.

I took the train to Southern Pines, several trains because I had to change in New York, and Grandfather and his chauffeur met me at the station. The service was at the Village Chapel, where Grandfather had given an organ in memory of Uncle Edgar.

There are no stained-glass windows in the chapel and I look out the clear windows at the pines as the minister talks about how much Grandmother did for the community of Pinehurst and what a fine Christian woman she was. I am sitting next to Mother and Annabel is squirming restlessly in her place beside Daddy. Aunt Edith's face looks more parchment yellow than ever under her black veil, but Jean wears bright red lipstick with the latest Chanel suit from Paris and ropes of pearls and gold chains that clink whenever she moves. The chapel is full of Grandfather and Grandmother's friends. Mother has told me that we will have to stand in line afterward and greet them all. The altar is covered with lavender flowers, Grandmother's favorite color, and I think how I will never see her again and tears come to my eyes and roll down my cheeks. I sniffle and Annabel turns and looks at me. Now the amethyst brooch will be mine, but I don't care. I would rather have Grandmother alive.

We go back to the house and Aunt Edith tells Mother about all the beaux who take Jean out and want to marry her and Mother says she doesn't think it's an appropriate subject to discuss at this time. Jean is twenty-two and her coming-out party was four years ago. I think Aunt Edith is anxious to get her married to someone with a title and that's why they take all those trips to Europe.

I wonder if I'll have beaux who want to marry me when I have my debut party in a few years? It would be awful to be a wallflower and not have anyone want you.

9

JEAN IS FINALLY GETTING MARRIED, and not to a duke or count but to a man who lies in New York named Fredric Gibson. She met him at a party in Southampton and he is an interior designer. Aunt Edith is very upset and she has been telephoning Mother to see what she can do to stop it.

"I'm sure he's after her money," she said. "And to think I had her presented at Court to have her throw herself away on this . . . this nobody!"

I overheard Mother and Daddy talking about it when I came home for Christmas vacation and Mother thinks it's out of spite, because two years ago Jean fell in love with a man who'd been divorced and Aunt Edith dragged her off to Europe for the summer and when they returned he'd married someone else. Jean was devastated and moped in her room for weeks and wouldn't speak to Aunt Edith.

"Serves Edith right," Daddy said. "She's always interfering in Jean's life."

Aunt Edith asked Grandfather to have a background check done on Fredric Gibson and when Jean found out about it she threatened to elope and Aunt Edith had to agree to the wedding.

Anyway, the wedding is going to be in April and I'm to be a bridesmaid. Annabel had a tantrum when she wasn't asked to be in the wedding, but she's too young to be a bridesmaid and too old to be a flowergirl. Jean showed me a picture of Fredric Gibson and he is very good-looking.

The wedding is in the garden of Aunt Edith's home in Winston-Salem and it looks beautiful with all the dogwood in bloom. Rows of white chairs are lined up for the guests and there is even a white piano rented especially for the occasion. Violinists are playing and Aunt Edith greets people as they arrive. She is wearing a long peach chiffon gown with a large hat and her diamond bar pin and a white orchid corsage, but her face has a pained expression as if making the best of a bad situation. Mother looks so pretty in a blue and lavender print and straw hat trimmed with a band of matching fabric and her pearl necklace. Grandfather isn't here because he is going to give Jean away and they will arrive shortly in the limousine.

Dark clouds are gathering in the sky, a bad omen, and several guests look up nervously as a rumble of thunder is heard in the distance. Maybe they should have rented a tent to be safe, but it is too late now. I hope the rain will hold off until the wedding is over.

But it doesn't. Suddenly the skies open and the rain pours down. The three violinists stop playing and rush inside, resembling fluttering hummingbirds as they try to protect their violins under their jackets, and the guests follow. A waiter gets a tablecloth and throws it over the piano but it soaks through immediately. Other waiters dash around moving tables and chairs into the house. Aunt Edith is wringing her hands. Not only are her dreams of Jean marrying into royalty destroyed, but her wedding is a shambles.

"What a disaster," she says. "And it all looked so lovely."

Just then the limousine arrives with Jean and Grandfather.

Fredric Gibson is waiting in the library with his best man, an actor he shared an apartment with in Greenwich Village.

Daddy takes charge of the situation as Aunt Edith rushes around talking to the caterers and directing waiters where to put the chairs.

"Come in out of the rain, everyone," he says. "We'll carry on as usual in a few minutes."

"There isn't enough room in the living room for all the guests," says Aunt Edith.

"Don't worry," Daddy assures her. "We'll manage all right."

So now they are to be married in front of the fireplace in the living room instead of under the wisteria arbor as we rehearsed. Nothing can be done about the white piano which is too heavy to be moved without piano movers and is getting ruined in the deluge. We'll just have violin music to march down the aisle to, and in half an hour everything has been moved inside and the wedding is ready to begin. The minister takes his place in front of the mantel and Fredric and his best man come out of the library, I take my bouquet of roses and snapdragons along with the other bridesmaids, and the music starts.

Jean and Fredric say their vows and I hear someone murmur what a handsome couple they make and what a shame that Randolph didn't live to see this day. The minister pronounces them man and wife, they kiss, then walk happily arm in arm down the aisle and we all follow.

Outside in the garden it is still pouring rain.

Several months later Mother and Daddy received a letter postmarked Reno. It was from Jean. Mother read parts of it to me.

"Dear Aunt Myra and Uncle Lamont,

You will no doubt be surprised to learn that I am in Reno so soon after my marriage. It seems the affection I longed for was not to be mine. Grandfather was right. I should have listened to him. I do not want to discuss it at this time but just want to pick up my life again.

I hope to see you when I get back. Give my love to Barbara and Annabel.

With my love,

Jean"

I was stunned. "What do you think happened?" I asked Mother.

She and Daddy exchanged knowing looks.

"It's a good idea when you marry to know the person for quite a long time and know something about their background," Daddy said.

Background. Grandfather was right. It must have to do with the background check that Grandfather had done on Fredric Gibson, something awful he found out, but Jean paid no attention and went ahead and married him anyway.

"Had Fredric Gibson been in prison or something?" I asked.

Again Mother and Daddy looked at each other and back at me. "No, he wasn't in prison," Daddy said.

"Then what?"

"I think you should ask Jean," Mother said. "If she wants to tell you. She may not."

Another mystery in the family. Like Uncle Edgar.

I decided to ask Lavinia if she knew about Jean and Fredric.

"Mother just got a letter from Jean from Reno, Nevada," I informed Lavinia, watching her reaction. "She's getting a divorce."

Lavinia rolled her eyes. "Don't surprise me none."

"You heard about it?"

"Not till just now. But all you had to do was take a good look at that man and know . . ." She stopped and took a frying pan out of the cupboard and put it on the stove.

"Know what?"

"There's some men who prefer other men to women."

"You mean he was . . . queer?"

"Don't know why them types bother to get married in the first place."

A horrible thought suddenly struck me. Was my beloved Uncle Edgar one of those? Was that why he drowned himself and why nobody wanted to talk about it?

"Lavinia, was Uncle Edgar. . . ?"

Lavinia looked at me without replying and then picked up an onion and started to chop it.

Yes, it all started to make sense, but still I didn't want to believe it. Mother's story about the porthole, how Uncle Edgar had opened it to get some air because his cabin had been freshly painted and fallen overboard. Even Kristin hadn't believed it when I told her. But it was a lie concocted to protect all of us and especially Uncle Edgar, so his image wouldn't be tarnished.

And what did men who were "queer" do anyway? I knew that many hairdressers and interior decorators were effeminate, obviously so, and people made jokes about them, but Uncle Edgar wasn't like that. He collected paintings and objets d'art and he liked to dress well, I had heard, and once Daddy referred to him as "a bit of a dandy." I remembered he had been taking what turned out to be his final cruise with another man. Was he his boyfriend? And what happened between them on the cruise? Did the other man want money, knowing he came from a wealthy family, and threaten to expose him, so that death was preferable to scandal? It was all forming a very unattractive picture.

"Now don't you tell your Mother we discussed this," Lavinia warned.

"I won't."

I wanted to cry, but there was only a pain deep inside of me.

10

"WOULD YOU LIKE TO GO WITH ME to see *Ecstasy* Saturday afternoon?" Sally asked.

"*Ecstasy*? Isn't that the movie that's for adults only?"

"Yes, but I'm sure we can get in if we dress up and wear a lot of lipstick."

I was curious to see it but I never would have gone by myself. At fifteen I had never been kissed and I had only vague ideas about sex. There were several girls at Farmington who were rumored to have "gone all the way" with a boy, but they were seniors and I had never talked to them. Another girl left school in the middle of the year and it was whispered that she was going to have a baby. She never came back.

"Do you think we could pass for sixteen? It would be embarrassing if they asked for proof and refused to let us in."

"Don't worry," said Sally. "Anyway, it's worth a try."

So on Saturday afternoon we dressed to look as sophisticated as possible with high heels and hats and dark lipstick. Mother had gone out for lunch with a friend and Daddy was playing golf at the Chevy Chase Club.

"Where are you going?" Annabel asked as I was leaving.

"To a movie with Sally."

"Can I come with you?"

"No."

"Why not?"

"You're too young. You stay here with Lavinia."

"I'm always too young to do things," Annabel said.

Sally and I walked over to Massachusetts Avenue to get the bus, tottering in our high heels and feeling very wicked. The theatre was downtown in an area near the burlesque houses and I was nervous when we got off the bus, especially when I noticed several shady-looking characters eyeing us. One man winked at me and I almost lost my nerve, but since we had come this far we might as well go through it.

Sally marched boldly up to the box office and handed her money to the cashier. "Two adults," she said.

The cashier looked us over suspiciously but gave her two tickets. There were photographs outside the theatre of Hedwig Kiesler, the leading actress, swimming nude in a lake and I remembered reading in the newspapers that her wealthy older husband, an Austrian munitions maker, had tried to buy up all the prints of the film.

Sally tugged my sleeve. "Come on." She lowered her voice. "It worked."

The movie had already started and it was so dark in the theatre that I didn't notice at first that there were only men in the audience. When I realized it I felt odder still. This would be an adventure I could tell the girls at Farmington about when school started again.

The movie was in German with English subtitles and Hedwig Kiesler was very beautiful. When it came to the famous nude scene Sally nudged me. The heroine ran through the woods, partly hidden by tree branches and bushes and swam in the lake.

A man in back of me said loudly, "No tits," and another

added, "Too big in the ass." Was this how men discussed women among themselves? I scrunched down in my seat embarrassed. Then there followed scenes of lovemaking done in close-up of the hero and heroine and they were nude but you couldn't see anything, only their heads and bare shoulders and backs. I couldn't figure out what they were doing, but from their expressions it looked as if they were in some kind of pain. The man beside me had his hand in his lap and was moving it back and forth rapidly and making low moaning sounds matching those on the screen and I wanted to get out of there and I wondered how Sally and I could sneak out before the lights came on. The theatre was filthy with discarded gum and candy wrappers tossed on the floor and smelled of stale chocolate and urine.

Finally it came to the end and Sally and I made a quick exit, hurrying as fast as we could to the bus.

"Well, we've seen it," Sally said. "What did you think of it?"

I didn't know what to say, not wanting to admit that I wasn't exactly sure what was going on in some of the scenes. "It was all right," I said.

"I thought it was pretty hot stuff," said Sally.

Several days ago I heard through a friend that Sally had died after a long bout with cancer. Our paths hadn't crossed for many years.

The beauteous Hedwig Kiesler signed a Hollywood movie contract and the studio changed her name to Hedy Lamarr. I saw all her movies and cut out pictures of her from fan magazines. I'd give anything to look like that, I thought, and after I saw her in *Algiers* I tried parting my hair in the middle and experimenting with different make-up in an attempt to resemble her, but it was no use. I was not a femme fatale.

By today's movie standards, *Ecstasy* would be considered

tame and no one would flick an eyelash at the famous nude scene or the simulated sex. But learning of Sally's death, it brought back memories of that Saturday afternoon so long ago, and of two innocent fifteen-year-old girls who thought they were being daring and wicked.

11

"IN THIS GRAVE HOUR, perhaps the most fateful in our history . . ."

King George is broadcasting from Buckingham Palace and we are all gathered in the library listening to it. Germany invaded Poland two days ago and then marched into France. The newspapers reported that the Duke of Windsor had sent a personal telegram to Hitler begging him to make every possible effort to keep peace, but Hitler did not reply. A Dutch steamer sailed from Amsterdam with five hundred Americans from all parts of Europe who were trying to get home in a hurry. I wonder if Aunt Edith is one of them?

"For the second time in the lives of most of us we are at war. . . ."

The words send a chill through me. England and France have declared war on Germany. Will we be drawn into it now? Daddy looks very serious as he listens. Mother fingers her pearls nervously and I remember her telling me that Daddy fought in the last war and was wounded in Belgium. He never talks about it and changed the subject when I mentioned it.

King George's speech is over and Daddy turns off the radio and goes upstairs.

"Where is Aunt Edith?" I ask Mother. "Isn't she in Europe?"

"I got a postcard from her several weeks ago from the Villa d'Este on Lake Como."

"Italy?"

"Yes." Mother looks worried. "But I'm sure she's left by now. I think I'll give her a call."

Aunt Edith and Jean divide their time between the house in Winston-Salem and the Fifth Avenue apartment overlooking Central Park that belonged to Uncle Edgar, and they're always taking trips, so no one is ever quite sure where they are at any given time. Uncle Edgar left the New York apartment to Mother as well, but she hates New York and never goes there. It suddenly occurs to me that now I won't be able to go to school in Florence next year the way I planned, unless the war is over by then, and it doesn't seem likely. I have to go back to Farmington in two weeks and I hate it there with the girls in their Brooks Brothers skirts and sweaters and polo coats and brown-and-white saddle shoes giggling about boys all the time, and I was looking forward to going to school in Florence at *La Petite Ecole*, where you speak French one week and Italian the next and where I could study the great works of art. Mother wants me to be a social butterfly and have a coming-out party, but I want to become an artist and I intend to.

There are air raids on London and British children are being evacuated to the country for their safety.

"Is Hitler going to come over here and bomb us?" asks Annabel.

"Don't be silly," I reply, but I am not so sure. Aunt Edith and Jean went on to Paris after Lake Como and sailed from Le Havre on the last French ship leaving Europe. The ship was packed and there weren't enough cabins and some people had to sleep in the lounge and on the decks. Aunt Edith told Mother it was a terrible crossing. If we get in the war, Daddy is too old to be called up, at least I think so. The whole thing is very frightening.

The news from Europe gets worse day by day. Italy has joined the side of Germany and it looks as if the war is going to last for a long time.

However life goes on as usual here. We look up at the skies nervously searching for enemy planes, but nothing happens.

In my dream bombs are exploding over Washington, blue and magenta with flashes of silver like fireworks, and Annabel is running through the garden with sparklers waving them in circles, her eyes glowing green in the dark like cat's eyes. The White House burns like cardboard, the Washington Monument explodes in fragmented pieces, and still the planes come, waves and waves of them. There is nowhere to run, nowhere to hide, and I hear a deafening roar in my ears as a bomb lands on the house next door, Sally's house, turning it into a pile of rubble.

"London Bridge is falling down, falling down, falling down," sings Annabel, and Princess Elizabeth and Princess Margaret Rose are in the dream too, but I'm not sure what they're doing. Another bomb explodes.

"Stop, stop!" I am screaming and tears are running down my face as Mother shakes me awake from my nightmare. Annabel is standing beside Mother in her printed Lanz nightgown rubbing her eyes.

"Barbara woke me up," she says. "She frightened me."

"It was only a bad dream." Mother puts her arm around Annabel and leads her back to her room.

I am busy packing my sweaters and skirts in my suitcase to go back to school when a telegram arrives with terrible news. Grandfather is dead.

He was killed by a disgruntled worker in one of his steel

plants who came to his office with a gun and shot him right in front of his secretary, then turned the gun on himself. I still can't believe it, and Mother is in a state of shock. Another tragedy in the family.

We are leaving for Pittsburgh tomorrow for the funeral and Aunt Edith and Jean are going to meet us. There are headlines in all the newspapers and the police say that the man who did it had a history of mental illness. I am worried about Mother, remembering how she collapsed after Uncle Edgar's death, and I wonder how she is going to get through it.

"Will Mother be left a lot of money?" Annabel asked me.

That thought hadn't even occurred to me, I was so upset about Grandfather. Annabel is always asking Daddy for things and he usually buys them for her. "I don't know," I said. "It depends on his will. I suppose his estate will be divided between Mother and Aunt Edith."

"Lavinia says they'll get a bundle."

"Perhaps he's left everything to charity," I said, irritated at Annabel. I would miss Grandfather. Now they are both gone, Grandmother and Grandfather, and they will lie side by side in the Pittsburgh cemetery where Uncle Edgar and my two aunts who died as babies are buried.

"Why don't we ever see Daddy's parents?" Annabel asked.

"Maybe we will now."

"They don't have much money, do they?"

"A lot of old Southern families lost their fortunes in the Civil War."

"I hope we don't lose ours," said Annabel. "I'd hate to be poor."

I realize I have not told much about Annabel and possibly I have blocked it out because it is too painful, but these memories come back because today is Annabel's birthday. We are not exchanging cards or gifts anymore after what she did with Mother's will, we are not even speaking.

Sometimes I wish we could erase the past and go back before everything happened between Annabel and myself, but it is not possible. There has been too much bitterness. I used to imagine Annabel and me as elderly ladies touring the English lake country, having tea and scones with jam and clotted cream in a charming inn and talking about the family the way we used to years ago. But it will never be. She used me, Annabel did, and then stuck a knife in my back. No, it wasn't as sudden or unexpected as a knife thrust, it was planned over years and years.

Then why didn't I see it? I always thought I was quite intelligent, I took pride in the fact that I could read people well. How could Annabel have fooled me so? I was too close to the situation, and yet also too far away, for I was the one who left, traveling to foreign lands, not seeing Mother that often when I was grown, while Annabel stayed in the same city, even after she married. She was able to keep an eye on things.

"I am provoked that Annabel is going into my financial affairs long before I have left this world," Mother wrote me in one of her weekly letters on the blue writing paper in her distinctive handwriting, letters that I have only to look at again to feel that she is still alive. Was it a cry for help that I did not recognize?

I see so many things in retrospect, now that Mother is gone.

12

IT STARTED LIKE ANY OTHER SUNDAY at boarding school, a day in December that would change all our lives. We were awakened to the sound of snow shovels clearing the walks and after breakfast we trudged through the wet snow to church, then lunch. I can still remember what we ate, pot roast with potatoes and carrots and stewed fruit for dessert. I was lying on my bed on the third floor of Colony House studying for the test in English history the next day and trying to get the dates of the wars set in my mind and the reigns of the various kings, when Sue Hancock burst in and announced, "The Japanese have just bombed Pearl Harbor!"

I started to shiver uncontrollably and I felt goose bumps up and down my arms under the two sweaters I was wearing. "How do you know?" I asked.

"It was on the radio just now. I was waiting for *The Shadow* to come on and they interrupted with a special bulletin. A lot of American ships have been sunk and thousands of people killed."

On Sunday afternoons at Farmington we usually listen to *The Shadow* and we all like the creepy stories and the eerie music and it is fun to go around imitating the sinister laugh and saying ominously, "The Shadow knows."

But this is real. War.

"I've got to tell everyone else," Sue said. "See you at dinner." She continued down the hall, the messenger of bad tidings.

I closed my book. I could no longer concentrate on English kings and dates. This is the news I have been dreading and now it is here.

At dinner everyone at the table is talking about it. Some of the girls have brothers or beaux who could be called up. I have neither, and Daddy is too old. Perhaps I am lucky.

"Your father went down to the War Department to offer his services," Mother wrote, "but he had a physical and the doctor found a heart murmur. He says it's nothing to worry about, and I don't know whether to be grateful he won't have to go to war or be concerned about his health. After all, I told him, he's over fifty, and he did his bit in the last war."

I was proud of Daddy for being so patriotic but I was thankful he wouldn't have to go overseas and fight. Mother said she was going to work for the Red Cross and Daddy had volunteered to be an air raid warden for our block. They looked forward to seeing me for Christmas vacation.

I shared a Diamond cab with three other people when I got off the train at Union Station. Mother apologized for not sending the Cadillac to meet me but there is a shortage of gas and everyone has to conserve.

Annabel is going to Potomac School and she announces at dinner that when she graduates she doesn't want to go to Farmington but to the Foxcroft School in Middleburg, Virginia, where they have horses.

"You would pick the most expensive boarding school, Annabel," Daddy says.

"I don't care. I want to go there," says Annabel.

After dinner we listen to Edward R. Murrow broadcasting from London. It sounds pretty scary there with all the bombs dropping. Daddy seems restless and keeps lighting cigarette after cigarette. I would like to ask him for one but I don't dare. We are not allowed to smoke at Farmington, but I have gone out in the woods with some of the other girls and tried one. It made me cough, but I felt very sophisticated.

Daddy grinds out his cigarette and pounds the arm of his chair. "I feel so useless," he says.

"But being an air raid warden is very important to the home defense," Mother says quickly.

"That's for women and old men who can't fight."

Daddy gets up and pours himself a drink. I can see that he is itching to get into it, despite his age. The casualty lists are still coming in from Pearl Harbor and a good friend of Mother and Daddy's, a navy captain, was killed on the bridge of his ship. His son went to Potomac School with me.

Mother has rented the house in Pinehurst to two Army families who are stationed at Fort Bragg, so I guess we won't be going to North Carolina for spring vacation. She says that housing is hard to find and she wants to do her bit.

"But two families?" I ask.

"They are sharing the house," Mother says. "There are plenty of bedrooms."

"I hope they won't damage it," I say, and then realize that doesn't sound very patriotic. After all, they are fighting for our country. It is so hard to realize that we are actually at war.

Here is a photograph from the trunk of Mother in her Red Cross uniform looking very trim and efficient. I think she enjoyed those days because for the first time in her life she felt really useful. She was in charge of a canteen. From a pampered favorite daughter used to being treated like a princess to a woman who gave elaborate dinner parties for her husband and had governesses to take care of her children, a woman who never had a job or had to think about a career like the women of today, she now had a purpose in life. She looks at the camera with her chin raised, a confident expression in her eyes, her cap with the red cross pulled down over her short dark curly hair.

The air is more serious at Farmington now, though some girls are still planning to have their coming-out parties, in spite of the war. Maybe they think the war will be over by then, but I don't think so. Japanese forces have occupied Manila and General MacArthur's army has had to withdraw to Bataan. And the news from Europe is just as bad as that in the Pacific. It is a frightening picture and it is hard to concentrate on my studies. We are safe here at boarding school in this quiet village in Connecticut, but I worry about Mother and Daddy and Annabel in Washington and I hope Hitler won't bomb us the way he did cities in Europe.

Sugar and meat are rationed now, so it takes a long time to save up enough coupons for a cake or a rib roast. They are going to issue gas ration books by summer and we also have coupons for shoes and we can only get two pairs a year because they need the leather for boots for soldiers. Now the war is real, even though we aren't getting bombs dropped on us the way they are in Europe.

Daddy is going to London for a job with the O.S.S. It's all very secret and he can't talk about it except to say that it stands for Office of Strategic Services. Mother and Annabel and I are very worried but he seems elated and feels that he is finally doing his part.

I haven't been saying my prayers lately but I'm going to every night from now on.

13

STRANGE, HOW YOUR LIFE CAN CHANGE in a moment and turn everything upside down, and later on you say, "What if I hadn't gone there that evening? We never would have met."

But I did. And that is where I met Richard.

It was January 1943 and a friend of Mother's had arranged a dinner-dance at the Sulgrave Club so that some of the young officers stationed in Washington and nearby could meet some nice girls, since most of the boys we grew up with had gone off to war. I hesitated about going, but Sally said it would be fun, and besides it was patriotic.

"Maybe you'll meet someone really cute," she said.

I was nineteen and I had never been in love. When other girls talked about it I tried to imagine what it might be like. I had kissed a few boys on dates and necked with them in cars but nothing magical happened. Suppose it never did?

"All right, I'll go," I said.

The Sulgrave Club was where I was going to have my

coming-out party if it hadn't been for the war. It looked very festive with flags and balloons and Sidney's orchestra playing. The ballroom was filled with officers and Mother's friend, Mrs. Breckinridge, was acting as official hostess.

"Barbara and Sally, how nice you could come," she said. "I want you to meet some of these fine young men." With that she pulled two naval lieutenants out of the stag line. "You introduce yourselves and enjoy dancing to this wonderful orchestra," she said and was off.

It was hard making conversation with someone I didn't know anything about and he wasn't a very good dancer but I tried my best. As we whirled around the ballroom I saw a handsome Army officer watching us. Then he walked over and tapped my partner on the shoulder.

"Guess I'll have to relinquish you to the Army," said the Navy lieutenant, whose name I had already forgotten. "Thanks for the dance."

I smiled and nodded politely and my new partner took me in his arms. He was much taller than the Navy lieutenant with brown eyes and dark hair and he had silver bars on his shoulders and infantry insignia on his lapels.

"I'm Richard Prescott," he said. "I noticed you when you first walked in, but the Navy beat me to it."

"I'm Barbara Ashford. Are you stationed in Washington?"

"Fort Myer. At least until my unit goes overseas."

"Where are you from?"

"Philadelphia."

The orchestra changed to a tango.

"I'm no good at these Latin dances," he said. "How about sitting down somewhere so we can talk?"

"There's a card room. We could sit there."

"Fine."

He took my arm and led me off the dance floor. I saw

Sally dancing with a marine and as we passed she gave me a wink.

"Your friend seems to be enjoying herself," Richard said.

"Sally always has a good time. She lives next door to me. We've been best friends since we were children." Now why was I telling him so much about Sally? Maybe he wanted to meet her. Sally's vivaciousness and devil-may-care attitude has always attracted boys while I was more quiet and serious.

The card room was adjoining the ballroom and we sat down at one of the tables. He asked me about my family and I told him that Daddy was in London with the O.S.S. and that Mother was an air raid warden and also did volunteer work for the Red Cross and I did too.

"Are you an only child?"

"No, I have a younger sister. Annabel."

"Is she as pretty as you?"

I didn't know how to answer that. Annabel was thirteen and at an awkward stage.

"I'm sure she couldn't be," Richard said.

He told me about his family in Philadelphia. He had a brother who was a priest, another who was studying to become a doctor, and two sisters. It was amazing how easy it was to talk to him and I felt as if I had known him all my life. I wondered how soon he had to go overseas and I hoped it wasn't soon. Could I be falling in love? Is this how it happens?

People were coming back from the buffet with plates of food.

"Are you hungry?" Richard asked.

"Yes, it looks good."

"Better than what we get at Fort Myer." He grinned. "Let's go."

When we returned with our food our table had been taken, so we looked for another place to sit.

"I have to get back to the base early," Richard said. "But I'd like to see you again. Would you give me your phone number so I can call you?"

I was so afraid he wouldn't ask.

After he left I danced with other officers, but none of them was as attractive as Richard. I hoped he meant it when he said he'd call me.

"It's June in January because I'm in love, and only because I'm in love with you." The next day I go around the house singing and Annabel asks me what's wrong with me.

"Bing Crosby sounds better on that record than you do," she adds.

I don't care. Richard, Richard. He is so handsome and I wonder if it is just the uniform, but no, he looks like Tyrone Power.

The telephone rings and I dash for it before Lavinia can answer it. It is Richard. He wants me to have dinner with him tomorrow night.

I change what I am going to wear three times and nothing looks quite right. Finally I put on the first dress I tried on and have just dabbed perfume behind my ears and checked to see if my stocking seams are straight when the doorbell rings.

He is here! Lavinia lets him in and I introduce Richard to Mother and I see her looking him over as if she wonders about his social background and Annabel is leaning over the bannister trying to peek at him and then I hear her singing "June in January" and I'd like to strangle her.

"Have a nice evening," Mother says, and we go down the front steps.

"I managed to borrow a car," he says, as we get in.

We have dinner at a little restaurant in Georgetown.

"You're the kind of girl I'd like to marry," Richard says,

leaning across the table, and I wonder how everything could be happening so quickly. Is it because of the war and the sense of urgency that hangs over everything, the desire to grab happiness now before it is swept away?

"How can you know? You've only just met me!" I remember something Daddy told me about not letting a man be too sure of you.

"I know all I need to know," Richard says.

It was like a scene from a movie, yet I was living it. I had someone to belong to now, someone who loved me. But he was going away, he was leaving in a few months to fight in the war and there was nothing I could do to prevent it.

Daddy is coming home from London and Richard and I are going to have a small quiet wedding with Annabel as my maid of honor and no other bridesmaids. I debated whether to ask Jean to be a bridesmaid, but I would rather have Sally and some of my friends, and since I can't have them it's better if I just have Annabel and no one else.

I can't believe I am really getting married!

Richard is a Roman Catholic and if we get married in a Catholic church I will have to have instructions from the priest on what it means to marry a Catholic and Mother and Daddy are upset enough about my marrying a Catholic, so we are going to be married in the library by an Episcopal minister from St. Thomas Church where I was confirmed. I guess his parents are upset too that I'm not a Catholic, but I'm sure that won't be a problem. The important thing is that we love each other.

"Dearly beloved, we are gathered here in the sight of God, and in the face of this company, to join together this man and this woman in holy matrimony. . . ."

I look up at Richard and think how handsome he is in his

uniform with the silver bars and how lucky I am to have met him. Annabel is holding my bouquet and I notice that Mother has tears in her eyes. Like Aunt Edith, did she imagine a more brilliant marriage for me to a Biddle or a Vanderbilt? But Richard is the man I want and we are going to be happy together forever and forever.

Forever was two months. That is all the time we had together in a rented apartment before Richard got his orders to go overseas.

It is our last night and we cling to each other as if we have no past and no future, only the present and these precious moments that all too soon will vanish. War. I try to blot the word from my mind as if it doesn't exist.

"Don't worry," Richard says. "I've too much to live for now that I've found you."

I hold him tighter. I try to assure myself that everything will be all right, that Richard will return safely, but deep down I am terrified.

Richard is stationed somewhere in England. I write to him every day but I don't know how many of my letters get through. I have started to number them so he will know if any are missing. He doesn't say much about what he's doing, just that he misses me.

I cannot stand being apart from him and it will be months or even years. At night I sleep with my arms wrapped around the pillow and try to pretend it is Richard. It doesn't work.

I am back living at home now in my old room and Annabel is going to Miss Madeira's as a day girl. It seems strange to be here with Mother and Daddy now that I am married. Annabel didn't get her way about going to Foxcroft. I think Mother favored it but Daddy said that Madeira was better academically if Annabel wanted to go to college. Two large buses pick up the fifty day girls at the Q Street bridge and drive them to Greenway, Virginia, to join the boarders.

I am lying on my bed looking at my wedding pictures when Annabel comes in my room and I notice that she is wearing one of my sweaters over her green Madeira uniform.

"What are you doing with my sweater?" I ask, annoyed that she just took it without asking.

She looks indignant. "You told me I could have it."

"No, I didn't."

"Yes, you gave it to me."

"When?"

"Last week. I asked you if I could have your sweater and you nodded and said 'All right' so I took it."

"I don't remember that at all."

"Maybe you didn't hear me. You were probably mooning over Richard."

I glare at her.

"But I did ask."

"I'd like it back. And please don't take anything else of mine without telling me."

Annabel took off the sweater and threw it on the bed. "There. You can have your old sweater." She went out, slamming the door.

I closed the wedding album. She was probably right and I was thinking about Richard and didn't hear her. I was worried sick about him. Our troops were going to have to invade France and I was sure that Richard would be part of that invasion. Naturally he didn't say anything in his letters and if he had they would be censored, but I felt certain that was why his infantry unit was in England.

That night I had a dream of Uncle Edgar. He was in army uniform getting out of a landing barge onto a beach and gunfire was coming from high cliffs above where machine guns were mounted. He was leading his men, trying to get them to follow him, and then he was hit and fell face down and the water washed over him and the water was bloody.

Uncle Edgar, Uncle Edgar . . .

But it wasn't Uncle Edgar. When one of his men turned him over and I saw his face, it was Richard.

More months dragged by, a year passed, the waiting seemed endless. I tried to keep busy with Red Cross work and not worry, but nothing helped. The invasion has to be soon, I thought. I wanted it to be over and Richard home and safe.

"INVASION!" screamed the headlines. "ALLIED LANDINGS BEGUN IN FRANCE, EISENHOWER SAYS."

It is Tuesday morning the sixth of June and the long-awaited invasion is now taking place. As I listen to the news on the radio I am paralyzed with fear about Richard, especially after my dream.

And then one terrible day it came. The yellow telegram, the messenger of death. Just like Uncle Edgar, only this time it was Richard. I read it over and from then on I heard nothing, I saw nothing, I felt completely numb. I must have gone into shock, because even now when I try to recall that moment and the time that followed, there is a huge blank.

Many years later I visited the Normandy beaches where the Allied landings took place. I was on a small Greek cruise ship sailing up the rivers and canals of Belgium and France. At Caen we were given a choice of an excursion to see the Bayeaux tapestries or Omaha Beach and the American Military Cemetery. I hesitated, then signed up for the latter.

It was a sunny August afternoon, and as we drove through the peaceful countryside with fields of corn and haystacks and pale brown Norman cows, it was hard to believe that this had once been a battlefield. The road was narrow and winding with glimpses of the sea from time to time. We passed a pretty stone church and a graveyard with flowers, vegetable fields, black-and-white cows, an old stone house with a gray slate roof and red and green ivy climbing its walls. Then suddenly the pastoral scene was broken by the sight of a former German bunker and beyond that a tall statue of the Virgin Mary with arms outstretched toward the sea.

"Thirty-five thousand soldiers landed on Omaha Beach," our tour guide said. "They had to wade ashore through rough seas carrying heavy packs and many were drowned. Because of the steep cliffs they had to scale and the high rate of casualties it was called 'The Bloody Beach.'"

I shivered. Omaha Beach was where Richard fell in the first assault wave. I wondered if I would be able to take this and if I should have opted for the Bayeaux tapestries instead. Ahead was a sign: American Military Cemetery, 7 km. We were almost there.

We entered the cemetery and got out of the bus. At first glance it looked like a vast garden with many trees and flower beds, but beyond lay Omaha Beach and row after row of white crosses, as far as the eye could see. A hush came over the group and no one spoke.

I walked away from the rest to look for the cross with Richard's name. Wind whistled through the pine trees and a white seagull was wandering among the crosses. Finally I found Richard's grave and I stood before it and remembered our brief months together. Tears welled up in my eyes. This was where it ended, our dreams, our future, and again I wondered about life and if it was all predestined or if it was merely chance that one man lived while another died. How different my life would have been if Richard had come back. But it was not to be.

Opposite a large pond of water lilies was the war memorial and I read the inscription:

THIS EMBATTLED SHORE, PORTAL OF FREEDOM, IS FOREVER HALLOWED BY THE IDEALS, THE VALOR, AND THE SACRIFICES OF OUR FELLOW COUNTRYMEN.

An elderly man wearing a cap looked at it and wiped his eyes. He seemed to be all alone and I couldn't tell if he was American or French. I noticed many French families here in the cemetery with their children.

The bells chimed from a nearby church. Five o'clock, time to leave. I walked back to the bus to join the others, glad now that I had come and made peace with my memories of Richard.

14

I DON'T KNOW WHAT TO DO with this photograph of Annabel taken by Bradford Bachrach in her wedding gown. In it she looks so sweet and innocent in white satin with a long tulle veil caught on each side with orange blossoms. She is holding her bridal bouquet and her only jewelry is a single strand of pearls and her diamond engagement ring. The photographer has retouched her nose and made it look almost retroussé when in reality Annabel has a sharp nose that is slightly crooked. She has not yet started to streak her hair and it is still light brown.

In the photograph her waist looks slim and no one knew that she was two months pregnant. Except Mother, who never let her forget it.

"Why did you tell her?" I asked later.

"I wish to God I hadn't," Annabel said.

Today, when unmarried couples are openly living together and movie actresses are having babies and not bothering to wed the father, it is hard to imagine what a scandal and disgrace it was in 1949 to be pregnant and unmarried.

I was in Paris studying art and trying to pick up my life after Richard's death when I got a letter from Mother.

"I don't want your father to know, but I am worried to death about Annabel," Mother wrote. "She is involved with a married man—a Chilean diplomat—and it can only lead to tragedy."

I wondered how Mother found out. Certainly Annabel wouldn't have told her.

"Perhaps you can talk some sense into her before it's too late," Mother concluded.

Me? Annabel had never listened to anyone when she wanted something. But I didn't like to think of Daddy's reaction. He still saw Annabel as his little girl and he might challenge the man to a duel. I decided to book passage for home as soon as I could.

However, before I could get back to Washington and offer Annabel my advice the diplomat's wife and child arrived from Santiago. End of the affair.

But Annabel was pregnant.

"I didn't want to have some back alley abortion," she told me later. So on the rebound she decided to marry Palmer Browne, a banker from an old Washington family who had been courting her and taking her to parties when she couldn't be seen openly with Miguel.

"I don't feel bells ring the way I did with Miguel," Annabel confided the night before the wedding. "But Palmer adores me and he's so good to me. He makes me feel safe and protected."

"But what about the baby?" I was horrified at the deception Annabel was planning.

"He'll never know. I'll just tell everyone the baby came early."

Annabel is walking down the aisle on Daddy's arm, an angelic smile on her face, as they approach the altar where

Palmer is waiting with his best man, his younger brother. In the front pew Mother holds her hands stiffly clasped, an orchid corsage pinned to her shoulder. Aunt Edith and Jean are on a cruise up the Nile and couldn't get back in time for the hastily-put-together wedding. I take Annabel's bouquet and she and Palmer kneel before the minister.

"Dearly beloved, we are gathered here . . ."

The familiar words bring tears to my eyes, remembering my own wedding to Richard in this same church five years ago. Do you ever get over someone you loved? I wondered. Would I ever meet any man who could make me feel the same way again? The few brief affairs since his death had left me feeling emptier than ever.

I looked at Palmer, whose eyes never left Annabel, as if he couldn't believe his good luck. Palmer appeared to me the kind of man who was very composed on the surface but who could explode in a deadly fury if crossed. I hoped that he would never find out that the baby Annabel was carrying wasn't his.

The following evening, after Annabel and Palmer had taken off for a two-week honeymoon in Bermuda, I was sitting in the library talking to Mother and Daddy. It was then I noticed for the first time how much Daddy had aged during the two years I'd been living in France. His hair was streaked with gray and he'd developed a paunch. Mother looked much the same, a few more lines around her eyes, but there was no gray in the short wavy brown hair.

"Well, that's over," Mother said with a sigh.

"What's that?" Daddy had *The Evening Star* turned to the financial page.

"Annabel's wedding."

"Oh, yes." Daddy lit another cigarette. "I wonder why they were in such a rush? We knew each other for several years before we got married. They were barely engaged."

I wondered if Daddy suspected the truth, but then Mother

said quickly, "You know how young people are today, Lamont. And we do know the family. I think Annabel realized that Palmer would make a nice stable husband."

I remembered what Annabel had told me the night before the wedding and I wondered if she was thinking of Miguel while she was on her honeymoon with Palmer. It would be impossible for me to marry a man I wasn't in love with, no matter how nice or stable or how much he adored me.

"There's something about that young man I don't like," Daddy said.

"Well, I think he'll be good for Annabel," said Mother. "He'll make her settle down." Lavinia came in with coffee on a silver tray. "Thank you, Lavinia, you can set it down right here."

I put two lumps of sugar in my cup and stirred the cream until it dissolved.

"I wish you could find someone to make you happy, Barbara," Mother said. "Why don't you stay on in Washington and see some of your old friends again?"

"That's a good idea," said Daddy.

"Madge Breckinridge has a very attractive nephew who works for the State Department. She was telling me at the wedding how pretty you looked."

"I know you both mean well, but I want to go back to Paris and continue my art studies. My teacher says I'll be ready for a showing soon. And I'd like to go to Italy and then perhaps Greece."

"But . . ."

"Mother, please let me run my own life. I'm not a child anymore."

"Barbara, your mother isn't trying to interfere in your life. And we both want what's best for you."

Now they were alone together with both their daughters gone, facing old age. I felt sorry for them but I couldn't live my life to please them.

"I have to do what I must do," I said. "I believe I have talent and I want a career as an artist. I've wanted it ever since I was a little girl."

"But that isn't enough," Mother said. "A woman needs a husband and children to make her life complete."

"Maybe Annabel will have a child and then you can be grandparents."

Mother looked at me sharply, as if she wondered if I knew the truth about Annabel.

"Annabel and Palmer are going to live in Washington and I'll be coming back often to visit." I felt stifled, like something being poured into a mold. I had to get back to Europe, to lead my own life the way I wanted.

Two days later I returned to Paris.

15

MOTHER WRITES that Jean is getting married again. Aunt Edith isn't pleased with this one either, according to Mother, and all the trips to Europe didn't turn up a titled husband. But Jean is getting on and wants children before it's too late. Somehow I can't picture Jean as a mother.

A letter from Annabel says that she and Palmer have bought "a darling house" on Waterside Drive overlooking Rock Creek Park, within walking distance of our house on Tracy Place. She says she envies me being in Paris and hopes that she and Palmer can take a trip to Europe after the baby's born. She sounds as if she's settled into married life and has forgotten all about Miguel. For her sake, I hope so.

Another letter from Annabel. "I have a little girl, nine pounds, four ounces, but of course I can't brag about her size, under the circumstances, and have to pretend that she's premature. She's so cute! Her name is Gillian and I want you to be her godmother."

I am an aunt. Strange, that Annabel, who is six years

younger than I, should be the first to have a baby. I wonder if I will ever get married again and have a child. But I am eager to see Gillian and hold her. My little niece. It reminds me of my childhood when I waited so eagerly for a sister.

Mother, I'm sure, is worried that her friends will start counting and add up that Gillian was born less than seven months after the wedding. She sets great store by what people think. As for me, I couldn't care less. Well, I guess that isn't strictly true, though I would like to think so.

In the letter I note that Annabel says, "I have a little girl," and not we, but of course that's the way it really is, and I wonder again about Palmer and if he has been completely deceived. It doesn't appear to bother Annabel.

"Of course you're coming home for the christening," Mother writes. "It's going to be in the Washington Cathedral with Dean Sayre officiating. As you know, he's the grandson of Woodrow Wilson."

This fact seems to impress Mother, who has been very active raising money to finish the cathedral and is on the board. She has even given a stained-glass window in memory of Grandfather. Mother is the letter writer in the family, but every once in a while I get a letter from Daddy.

As I make my reservations to sail home for the christening, I keep wondering what Gillian looks like. I hope she doesn't resemble Miguel!

✻ ✻ ✻ ✻ ✻

Annabel hands me Gillian and I give her a kiss and rock her in my arms. "She's adorable," I say. Her eyes are hazel and her dark hair looks as if it's going to be curly.

"Palmer thinks she looks like his mother," says Annabel.

"That's lucky."

Annabel gives me an angry look.

"Sorry, I didn't mean anything. By the way, what's ever happened to Miguel?"

"He's in Madrid." Annabel rips open a large bundle wrapped in blue paper and starts to fold the diapers that have come back from the diaper service. She seems restless. "I hear his wife is expecting a child." She tosses it off as if the wife has gotten pregnant by remote control and I suddenly wonder if Miguel is the reason she wants to go to Europe. That would really be playing with fire.

Gillian wrinkles up her nose and lets out a loud wail.

"Time for her bottle," Annabel says. "I'll get it."

"Aren't you nursing her?"

"Hell, no! I don't want to end up with sagging breasts. And Mother always made such a big deal about nursing us that the whole idea just turned me off. Besides, my doctor says it doesn't make any difference."

I pick up a rattle and attempt unsuccessfully to quiet Gillian while Annabel goes down to the kitchen to heat her bottle.

In a few minutes Annabel returns with the bottle. "Would you like to give it to her?"

"All right."

"Sit in this chair." Annabel indicates an armchair and drapes a diaper over my shoulder. "That's in case she throws up any milk. And you have to burp her every two ounces so she doesn't get gas in her stomach."

Gillian is so small and I'm afraid I won't do it right. "Perhaps you'd better," I say, holding out Gillian to her.

"No, you do it. It's good practice for when you have your own."

Again it seems strange to me that my little sister should be teaching me how to feed a baby, but I take the warmed bottle that Annabel hands me and put the nipple in Gillian's mouth.

"See, it's simple," says Annabel.

We hear the front door opening and a man's voice calls up the stairs, "Honey, I'm home." It's Palmer returning from the Riggs Bank at Dupont Circle where he is a vice-president in the trust department.

"Hello, darling." Palmer kisses Annabel and I notice that she responds without enthusiasm, but maybe it is because I am here. "How are you, Barbara? Good to see you again." Palmer gives me a perfunctory kiss on the cheek, then pats Gillian. "What do you think of our pride and joy?"

"She's enchanting."

"Yes," Palmer agrees. "Not bad for a first try. The next one will be a boy."

"Next one!" Annabel gasps.

"I meant in a year or two, not right away."

"I should hope so. I've barely gotten my figure back."

Palmer gives her a playful swat on her rear. "You look fine."

Palmer is not my idea of every woman's dream come true and I have visions of him reading bank reports in bed, then turning and saying, "What position shall we try tonight, dear?" But he seems devoted to Annabel and I guess that is what's important. I am probably too romantic and idealistic.

"I'll fix us a drink," Palmer says.

"Good, I can use one," says Annabel. "We'll be down to join you as soon as Gillian finishes her bottle. Oh, we're having dinner with Mother and Daddy at the Sulgrave Club at eight," she calls after him.

Mother and Daddy and I are in the living room, sitting on the ivory brocade loveseats in front of the fireplace having a pre-dinner drink before going to the Sulgrave, while we wait for Annabel and Palmer.

"They're late as usual," Daddy says, lighting another cigarette.

"Lamont," Mother warns, her eye on the cigarette, "remember what your doctor told you."

"Hell, if I can't do what I enjoy anymore, I'd rather be dead!" Daddy inhales a deep puff of smoke and blows it out.

"He didn't say you had to completely cut out smoking and drinking, just cut down."

"I don't trust a man who won't have a drink," Daddy says.

Above the mantle is a painting of *Master Kemble* by John Hoppner, a beautiful young boy in a velvet suit and lace collar with long curls and an angelic expression.

"I've always loved that painting," I say, glancing up at the Hoppner.

"Yes, so do I," Mother says. "I must have it cleaned. The National Gallery gave me the name of a man they recommend, but it takes several months and I don't like the idea of that blank space for so long."

The doorbell rings and Lavinia goes to get it. Lavinia has put on weight since I last saw her and her hair is streaked with gray now but she is still with us. It would be odd to think of the house without her, she is so much a part of my childhood. Strange how you can go away and live in another place, even another country, but you want your childhood home and the secure things you remember to stay the same.

"We're here," Annabel announces. "Sorry we're a little late."

"We'd better go on now to the Sulgrave Club and have another drink there," Daddy says.

"Good idea," says Palmer.

Today a certified letter came from Annabel. As I signed for it, I wondered what she could be writing about, since we've only communicated through lawyers for the past year.

"As the bank probably informed you, I've been trying to sell Mother's Hoppner painting and have had it in several auctions but the offers we got were so ridiculous that I withdrew it," Annabel writes. "I've tried several galleries as well and they weren't interested. They wouldn't even give us three thousand dollars for it and were of the opinion that when it was cleaned the man ruined it. What do you think we should do? Please let me know as soon as possible."

There was a P.S. "I've had some family photographs copied for you and you were going to have copied the one of Mother in the silver frame that you took."

Incredible that Annabel would write to me as if everything is normal, as if she hadn't taken Mother's will and stolen most of her bonds. Is she getting worried now that the government is on the trail and closing in?

I don't want the Hoppner now. The man who cleaned it one summer when Mother and Daddy went to Europe returned a painting with a completely different expression. I don't know whether he used a solvent that was too strong, but instead of the formerly sweet expression, Master Kemble now has a nasty smirk.

And I think how the Hoppner painting resembles Annabel, with the angelic expression on the outside and the real one underneath, the one I never saw until Mother died.

How could I have been so blind?

But Annabel was my sister and I loved her. In an odd way, in spite of everything, I guess I still do.

16

IT HAPPENED LIKE THE LINE from a song, a stranger across a crowded room. I noticed him first, the intense-looking man with dark hair, an unruly lock falling over one eye that he kept pushing back with his hand as he talked, or rather argued with another man, and more people at the party wandered over to join in the discussion.

"Who is he?" I asked John, a friend of a friend I'd gone out with several times who was nice but unexciting.

"Darren McLeod. Paris correspondent for the *Washington Post*."

"He looks interesting."

"Want to meet him?"

Just then he looked over and waved to John.

"Is he married?"

"No. Darren never stays in one place long enough. He likes covering wars and riots."

"It doesn't sound as if he'll have a very long life at that rate," I said, and wondered if I was inwardly drawn to danger or men who liked it. I didn't have time to contemplate that when Darren McLeod walked over to us.

"Well, John, how do you rate getting the best-looking broad in the place?" He fixed me with a stare.

"Barbara Ashford, Darren McLeod," John said. "And the lady isn't a broad."

"Sorry. I meant it as a compliment."

John took my glass. "I'll go freshen our drinks."

"So, Barbara Ashford, what brings you to Paris in the winter?"

"I've lived here for three years. I'm a painter."

"What do you paint?"

"Landscapes mostly. Some portraits. Whatever inspires me."

"I'd like to see your work."

"I'm having a showing next week at the Gallerie Laffont if you'd like to come."

"Wish I could, but I'll be in Berlin then." He took out a small black book. "Give me your home phone number and I'll call you when I get back."

Just then John returned with our drinks and Darren said he had an assignment to cover.

"Nice meeting you, Barbara Ashford," he said. "Behave yourself, John." He grinned and was gone.

Six weeks passed and I had given up on hearing from him when the phone rang late one evening.

"I didn't know if I'd find you home at this hour," the man's voice said. "Darren McLeod. Remember, the party?"

"Oh, yes. You were going to Berlin."

"I'm back and going to Rome next week. You've probably already had dinner, but can you have a drink with me?"

"Tonight?"

"Yes. Sorry my work doesn't allow me to give more advance notice."

"Where?"

"The Ritz bar in an hour?"

"I think I can make it."

"Good. I'll be waiting for you."

It felt strange walking into the Ritz bar all alone at eleven in the evening and at first I didn't see him. Then he spotted me and came over.

"I have my usual table in the corner," he said, taking my arm. "My second office."

There was a half-empty glass at the table. "I thought I'd have to have several of these before you appeared. Most women when you say an hour take at least two." He offered me a cigarette and lit it, then took one for himself. "What will you have to drink?"

"A Dubonnet."

"Waiter, another Scotch and a Dubonnet for the lady." He turned back to me. "How did the showing of your paintings go?" he asked.

"Very well. The critics were kind and I sold several."

"Congratulations."

"Thank you. How was Berlin?"

"Fascinating. I got a couple of good stories."

"There are rumors that Hitler is still alive."

"Not true. Though some of those Nazis escaped to South America." The waiter put the drinks down and Darren raised his glass. "Good health. Or as the Chinese say, 'May you live in an interesting time.'"

I took a sip of my Dubonnet.

"So, tell me about yourself," he said. "We didn't have a chance to cover much ground at the party."

"I grew up in Washington and went to school there. Potomac School. Then I went away to boarding school in Connecticut."

"Any brothers or sisters?"

"A younger sister. Annabel."

"And you always wanted to be a painter?"

"Ever since I can remember. Art was my best subject at school. In fact, the *Washington Post* published several of my drawings as a child. I don't know if a Sunday section called the *Junior Post* still exists."

"Not since I've been with them."

"It published poems and drawings of children. The cut-off age was fourteen. Anyway, when I was ten I did a pen-and-ink drawing of a little girl walking her dog and I sent it to the *Post*. My mother said they wouldn't publish it. So much for family support." I laughed.

"And they did publish it?"

"Yes. Two weeks later. I got up early before anyone else in the family that Sunday and when I opened the *Junior Post* section, there on page two was my drawing. It was the most exhilarating feeling! I woke up Mother and Daddy and showed it to them in triumph. After that I sent them other drawings and they published those too. I even won a prize of one dollar for the best drawing, a group of girls in their graduation dresses holding flowers."

"I know that feeling," Darren said. "I felt the same way when I saw my first story in print."

"You're not from Washington?"

"No, I grew up in Chicago, one of six children. My dad died when I was ten. It was the middle of the Depression and we were poor. I got a job delivering newspapers to help support the family and got attached to the smell of newsprint." He grinned. "Quite a different background from yours."

"How long have you been with the *Washington Post*?"

"Five years. I was a war correspondent, covered the D-Day landings." He suddenly noticed my expression. "Is something wrong?"

"My husband was killed on Omaha Beach."

"I'm sorry. I didn't know. Put my foot in it again."

"That's all right."

"They were heroes, those boys. Real heroes."

"We hadn't been married very long when he left. And then suddenly it was all over." He listened with interest and sympathy as I talked. I'd kept it inside for so long and it felt good to unburden myself to someone. I felt comfortable with him, as if I could say anything. "So I decided to bury myself in my art," I said. "I didn't think I could feel anything for any other man."

"And do you still feel that way?"

"I think the numbness is going away and I'm starting to come back to life."

"Good. How about dinner tomorrow night?"

And so it began. I found I was falling in love again. I met him in Rome and we walked holding hands along the Via Veneto. Later I threw a coin in the Trevi Fountain for luck.

"You must see the gardens and fountains at Tivoli," he said, and the next night after dinner we drove there and stood among the ancient trees and myriad fountains looking down on the lights of Rome in the distance.

Driving back he mentioned a girl he'd gone with for some time. "But she started talking about a rose-covered cottage and the patter of little feet," he said. "That's when I cut out. I'm not the marrying kind."

So he's warning me, I thought, in case I get the same ideas. I must be careful.

But when we made love I threw all caution to the winds. Nothing else mattered but being with him.

17

THE TELEPHONE CALL CAME without warning.
Mother was on the line, a poor connection, and at first I couldn't
understand what she was trying to tell me as she seemed to be
crying.

"Your father . . ." Then she broke down.

"Yes? I can't hear you very well."

"He's gone. He had a heart attack playing golf. He was at
the Chevy Chase Club and they called an ambulance right
away and rushed him to the hospital, but it was too late."

"Daddy . . ." I wanted to say it wasn't true but I knew it
was and I must be strong.

"It was one of those hot humid days and he wasn't feeling
well when he got up in the morning. I tried to persuade him to
cancel his game, but you know how he is."

Yes, I knew. "I'll be there right away," I said. "I'll get the
first flight available.

Daddy dead. The reality is slowly starting to sink in, but
I don't want to accept it.

Daddy . . .

"Lamont!" I hear Mother calling Daddy. He is outside with me pulling me on a red sled Santa Claus brought for Christmas. There is barely enough snow to make it go across the lawn but I want to ride on it anyway. The bushes have frost on them and my nose is red. I smell of wet wool and Vicks Vaporub. "Lamont!" Mother appears at the garden door. "Barbara has a cold. She shouldn't be outside in this weather."

"She just wanted to ride on her sled," Daddy said. "A few minutes won't hurt her."

All I have now are memories and I throw myself on the bed and cry until no more tears come. Then I pull myself together and make a plane reservation for the next day and leave a message for Darren at the newspaper office.

I get my suitcase and take some clothes out of my closet and start to pack but I am moving as if in a trance. Daddy gone. Daddy dead. It keeps repeating in my head like a metronome. At least it was quick and he didn't suffer, I try to console myself. It had to happen sometime. More tears come. I wonder if anyone is ever prepared? We think our parents will be here forever.

"Daddy!" It is like a strangled sob. "Come back!"

"I'm glad you're here," Annabel said. "Even though we thought when we were growing up that it wasn't a very happy marriage, they had more in common than we realized."

Forty years together. Over now.

"She depended on him," Annabel said. "Now she's alone."

How empty the house seemed without Daddy. I was half-expecting him to walk down the stairs, even though I knew he wouldn't. Ever. His body was lying in the mortuary and we would have to go and choose a casket and make the arrangements for the funeral services.

I wanted Darren here to hold me, to feel his arms around me, to comfort me.

"Palmer's been such a help," Annabel said. "He had to do all this when his father died. We have to be sure to get a lot of death certificates at the mortuary for the insurance and other things."

Of course. The insurance. Probate. The Internal Revenue. All those practical things. My mind didn't seem to be functioning clearly.

"Palmer said Daddy had a lot of insurance," Annabel said. "Luckily he got it before he started having trouble with his heart." I was starting to say something when Annabel said, "I hear Mother coming."

Mother came slowly down the stairs dressed all in black with a string of pearls. She looked very frail and was holding on to the bannister.

"I'm so glad both you girls are here with me," Mother said. "Maybe you'll think about moving back here now, Barbara."

I intended to return to Paris as soon as everything was taken care of. After all, Annabel was here and Mother had her two granddaughters, Gillian and Louise, to keep her company. I felt suddenly guilty, as if I should stay in Washington longer than the two weeks I'd planned.

"Yes, that would be fun," Annabel agreed. "Why don't you?"

"You can paint anywhere, can't you?" Mother said.

For a brief moment I was a little girl sending my drawing to the *Washington Post* and Mother telling me they wouldn't publish it. "It's a little more involved than that," I said, and just then the phone started to ring again. "I'll get it." I wanted to escape this conversation. I had my life now the way I wanted it, especially after meeting Darren, and I didn't wish it to change. Was that selfish of me?

It was a friend of Mother's who was on the board of the

National Symphony with her wanting to express condolences and asking about the funeral service. The obituaries in the newspapers hadn't said, just that funeral services were pending.

"I know Mother would like to talk to you," I said. "Let me get her."

Today is Daddy's funeral. It is early morning and already the heat and humidity promise to be unbearable. My clothes are laid out on the other twin bed in my room. Black bra and slip, beige panty girdle and black stockings, a black linen dress, black patent-leather pumps and a black straw hat with a veil.

I start to get dressed, but my clothes stick to me and beads of perspiration keep forming above my mouth and my makeup is running. I wash my face and start all over again but it isn't much better. It will have to do.

I don't feel a bit hungry but I guess I'll have to eat a little something or I won't be able to get through this. My eyes tear up again. Daddy dead. Daddy gone. I still don't want to accept it.

Mother is already up sitting in her usual place at the dining room table. I kiss her and sit down. Lavinia has a glass of orange juice at my place and I drink it.

"Annabel and Palmer will be here in an hour," Mother says. "And Jean and Bill. We'll all go together in the limousine to the cathedral."

Bill Persky is Jean's new husband. He works for the F.B.I. so they're living in Washington. "He's no better than a glorified cop," Aunt Edith told Mother. I guess she still had hopes of Jean being a countess or baroness.

"Is Aunt Edith coming?" I ask.

"No, she's not feeling well," Mother says, but I think the real reason is Bill Persky.

"What will you have for breakfast, Miss Barbara?" Lavinia asks. "Eggs and bacon?"

"No, just toast and black coffee."

"You'd better eat more than that," Mother says.

"That's all I want."

Daddy wanted to be buried in Charleston, so tonight we will accompany the coffin on the train to Charleston and tomorrow have a graveside service at the cemetery by the Ashford family plot. Daddy's parents are dead now, but I guess some of his cousins I've never met will attend.

After breakfast I go up to his room and sit on the heavy carved oak bed. On his bureau is his favorite photograph of Mother in an oval silver frame and pictures of Annabel and me as children. I bite my lip and tears fill my eyes. I must not break down, I tell myself. His suits are all hanging in his closet, his shoes lined up neatly in shoetrees, his ties on a rack. All these will have to be cleaned out, given to the Salvation Army or some charity. Annabel and I will have to do it because I know Mother won't be able to. I pick one of his ties, one I remember him wearing so often, a navy with narrow maroon stripes, and I take it to my room and put it in my suitcase.

"We'll have to decide what to do about the house," Annabel said, when we returned from burying Daddy in Charleston. "It's too big for just Mother and Lavinia to be rattling around in."

"Isn't that up to Mother to decide? This is her home and she's lived her for so many years. It's full of memories."

"Barbara, you're far too sentimental. We have to be practical and Mother's in no state to think clearly right now."

"She appears to me to be thinking clearly. Besides, they say that a widow shouldn't make any major decision for at least a year."

"Well Palmer says—"

"I'm tired of hearing about what Palmer says and thinks. He's not a member of the family."

"He was certainly a help during all of this. You seem to be going to pieces, Barbara."

"I'm sorry. I didn't mean it that way."

"After all, Lavinia's no spring chicken. I don't know how much longer she'll be able to go on working. And there's the house in Pinehurst. Mother and Daddy spent several months there each winter. It's fine for you. You go trotting back to Europe to do your painting and I'm stuck here with Mother and all her problems. It isn't fair."

It was me that Mother had leaned on during the funeral, not Annabel or Palmer, though she had walked down the aisle on Palmer's arm. Again I felt guilty. Maybe Annabel was right.

"Well let's discuss it with Mother and see what she wants to do about the house," I said.

"You know Mother and how hard it is for her to make a decision. She depended on Grandfather and then on Daddy and now they're both gone."

Yes, Mother was all alone now, the two most important men in her life dead. There would be terrible periods of loneliness ahead for her. Though she had her charities and her friends, I told myself, to fill her time. Still, it would be a difficult adjustment. "She could travel," I said.

"Mother wouldn't enjoy traveling alone."

"She could go with friends. And maybe she'll remarry."

Annabel looked as if she had been struck by lightning. "Mother remarry? At her age?"

"Many older women do. And Mother's still a very attractive woman."

"It would probably be to some fortune hunter who was after Grandfather's money," Annabel said.

Daddy hadn't left that much. I was surprised when the will was read and his safe deposit box opened how little there was. Apparently he had been speculating heavily on the stock market and had debts to be paid off. Mother had always kept her money separately, just like the separate bedrooms, though I had no idea how much she had.

"I think Mother should get a really top financial expert to handle her affairs," Annabel said. "Palmer knows someone, if we can persuade her to see him."

I realized that Annabel and Palmer had spent quite a lot of time discussing Mother's financial affairs, though perhaps that came naturally being a banker. I had never thought that much about money, as long as I had enough to live on, and I had never been extravagant.

"Let's talk to Mother after dinner and see what she wants to do about the house," I told Annabel. "It should be her decision."

✻ ✻ ✻ ✻ ✻

"I don't know, I just don't know," Mother said. "If I sold this place where would I go?"

"You have the house in Pinehurst," I said.

"But it isn't air-conditioned and it gets too hot in North Carolina after May to stay there. Besides, I have my friends in Washington, my charities. The cathedral, the symphony. . ."

"You could get an apartment in Washington, something that would be easier to maintain than this large house."

"Then what would I do with my furniture, all my lovely things?"

"You could use some things and store the rest," Annabel said.

"I don't want to think about it right now," said Mother.

Annabel threw me an I-told-you-so look. "You have to think about it sometime, Mother. And before Barbara goes back to Europe."

I thought Annabel could have omitted that last part. "Let's

let Mother decide what she wants to do, Annabel. After all, it is her house."

"I'm just trying to be helpful," said Annabel.

"Of course you were, dear, and I appreciate it," Mother said. "But it's too soon for me to think rationally about anything."

Warnings that I did not see, omens of things to come. I returned to Europe and Darren, leaving Annabel and Palmer in charge of Mother's affairs.

18

WE ARE GLIDING in a boat through the canals of Bruges, past windows with lace curtains and window boxes filled with geraniums. Ducks swim alongside us and I point out to Darren a restaurant with wooden shoes decorating a wall. Another has a terrace with white roses. Everywhere we see flowers, even planted in boxes along the canals. A horse-drawn carriage carrying a young couple with two small children crosses a picturesque stone bridge.

"I wish we could stay here longer than just the weekend," I say.

"It is beautiful here, isn't it," says Darren. "But perhaps that's part of its charm. We know we can't stay long enough to be bored."

He has a restless side that makes him always want to be in the thick of action, to be covering the latest war. I know that and his fearlessness makes him more exciting than other men, but it scares me a little too.

"I could never be bored anywhere with you," I say.

I'm in love with Darren and I think he loves me, but he is no closer to making a commitment than when we met. Yes, it's true he warned me in the beginning that he wasn't the marrying kind, but no woman ever believes that.

I could give him an ultimatum, but then I would have to face the possibility that he would walk away and I can't imagine life without him. He makes every other man seem dull.

So I will just wait and see what happens.

Annabel is expecting another baby. "I feel that this time it's a boy," she writes. "I'm carrying it differently." I think that's really an old wives' tale about how you carry a baby, but then I've never had one, and I hope for Annabel's sake that she has a boy. She writes that she and Palmer have bought an old house in McLean with lots of property and they are getting an architect to remodel it. "I *love* the Virginia countryside. I'm dying for you to see the place!"

And I think what different paths Annabel's life and mine have taken. I wouldn't be content to live in the Virginia countryside, no matter how pretty the landscape. I need Paris and Rome and the excitement of travel and seeing new places. In that way Darren and I are very much alike.

Mother wants to know if I'm coming home for Christmas and I write her that I will make my plane reservations. Maybe it will be good for Darren to miss me. It is the first Christmas since Daddy's death and I should I should go home, and I feel guilty about not wanting to.

Annabel has apparently been busy in my absence. After dinner Mother says, "I have something I want to show you. I told Annabel I wouldn't sign it until you came home."

"What is it?"

Mother hands me a legal-looking document. *I, Myra Calhoun Ashford, presently a resident of the District of Columbia, execute this affidavit under oath and say as follows*:

In it Mother stated that her late brother Edgar Calhoun

had neglected to put "and future issue" in his will when it was written, and she was certain it would have been his wish to have both her children treated equally, that it was her desire as well, and that she hoped the court would take this into consideration. As I read over the document I became very angry with Annabel.

"Mother, don't you see what this affidavit is? It's an attempt to change Uncle Edgar's will. I'm sure Palmer is behind all this."

"Palmer has been advising me about my financial affairs," Mother admitted. "After all, he *is* a banker, and it's so hard for a woman alone to know about these matters."

"Don't sign it. I want to discuss this with Annabel when she comes over tomorrow. Without Palmer," I added.

"About that affidavit you brought me to sign, Annabel," Mother said. "I don't know what to do. I wish your father were still alive. I want to be fair."

"But this *is* fair, Mother. What isn't fair is for Barbara to inherit all that money from Uncle Edgar when I don't get any of it."

"But you weren't born then, Annabel."

"I can't help that."

"And besides, your father and I have tried to even things out in our lifetimes. We've given you stock, bought you and Palmer your Washington house, and now this expensive place in McLean."

"It still isn't equal," said Annabel. "And Palmer agrees."

"I wanted to show this to Barbara since she was coming home, but I want to think it over about signing it. So I'll just put it in my desk for the time being."

Annabel scowled, two deep furrows appearing between her eyebrows and her mouth was set in a hard line.

"You and Palmer have rather extravagant living habits," Mother continued. "Barbara has never asked me for anything."

"I don't know how you can say anything against Palmer, Mother, when he was so helpful after Daddy died."

"Tell me about your new house in McLean," I say, trying to diffuse the situation, as I can see that Mother is getting very upset.

Annabel lightens up. "It's an old place that we're remodeling, and it has lots of ground for the children to play, which the little house on Waterside Drive doesn't. And we've found the most marvelous architect. I'll drive you out there. You'll love it. Mother thinks we got in over our heads, but it has such possibilities. And with three children we need a bigger place."

"It's going to cost a fortune to heat that house in the winter," Mother says.

Annabel ignores this. "Why don't we drive out now?" she says. "Then we'll be back in time for dinner."

"All right."

"Would you like to come with us, Mother?" Annabel asks.

"No, thanks. You girls go on and I'll see you later."

"Honestly," Annabel said, as she got in the station wagon and settled herself behind the wheel, "all Mother does is complain about spending. You'd think she was a pauper."

"It's got to be difficult for her adjusting since Daddy's death. You have Palmer and Gillian and Louise and the new baby coming, and she's all alone with Lavinia."

"You have to admit Mother's never been easy to live with and she's getting worse. You're damned if you do and damned if you don't," Annabel said. "Anyway, I can't wait for you to see the house. We really got it for a steal, because it does need a lot of work. But there's an old mill with a waterfall and a pond with ducks and acres of land."

"Sounds nice."

"It is. I was hoping it would be finished by the time the

baby was born, but I'm told these things always take longer than you plan. I hope Hugh's there."

"Hugh?"

"Hugh Langston, the architect. He's so handsome. Wait till you meet him. And he plays polo."

What did playing polo have to do with designing the house? I wondered, and a warning bell rang in my head. It was all sounding faintly familiar. "What do you have to do to the house?" I asked.

"It needs all new wiring and we're knocking out the living room ceiling and making it a cathedral ceiling. That will take away two of the bedrooms above it, but we're building a new wing. And of course all the bathrooms need remodeling and I'm going to have a real country kitchen, the kind I've always wanted. We're knocking out the wall to the laundry room and combining it into one room, because the original kitchen was tiny and cramped and this new one will be very spacious with knotty pine cabinets and hand-hewn beams on the ceiling and a copper hood over the stove with lots of copper pots and pans hanging on racks and a round oak table in the center of the room so we can eat breakfast there and informal suppers."

"It sounds as if it's going to cost a fortune."

"Now you sound just like Mother," Annabel says. "You have to spend money to have nice things. Mother's still living in Grandfather's time when you paid the help a dollar a day. She has no idea what things cost today."

I look out the window at Rock Creek Park. The trees are bare and the sky is gray with a few dark clouds. Washington always used to depress me in the winter and I couldn't wait for spring when the daffodils and crocuses burst forth and the dogwood and cherry blossoms.

"You like living in Paris, don't you?" Annabel said.

"Very much."

"Is there any special man in Paris?"

"Yes, there is someone. He's a journalist." And I told her about Darren and how we'd met.

"He sounds interesting."

"He is. But there's no future to it. He's not the marrying kind."

"Most men say that. Until they're caught."

The idea of setting a trap for a man seemed very unappealing to me. And dishonest. I wanted Darren to want me because he couldn't live without me, not because I'd tricked him. "I don't like playing games," I said.

"That's part of the fun," said Annabel.

We were passing the Lincoln Memorial and heading toward the Chain Bridge and Virginia.

"The great thing about McLean," Annabel said, "is that it's not far from Washington but it's like living in the country. We looked at places in Middleburg but decided that it was too much of a commute every day for Palmer."

I remembered that Annabel had wanted to attend Foxcroft School in Middleburg, the most expensive of all boarding schools.

"Anyway," said Annabel, "this fabulous house in McLean came on the market. It was a probate and the estate was eager to sell quickly."

We were in Virginia now and I looked at the houses and wondered what it would be like to live here. I'd lived in an apartment for so long.

"It looks a bit dreary now," Annabel said. "But you should have seen the countryside in October when all the leaves were gorgeous colors."

She rounded a curve in the road and turned up a long winding driveway. "This is it."

I saw the pond with ducks and the old mill with the waterfall and a rambling house set up on the hill. There were several workmen's trucks parked in the driveway and as we pulled up in front of the house a man came out and started to get in a red truck.

"Hello, Bill." Annabel waved. "That's my contractor."

Bill walked over to us. "Hello, Mrs. Browne."

"This is my sister who's visiting from Paris," Annabel said. "I want to show her the house."

"Pleased to meet you," Bill said.

"How's everything going?"

"All right." Bill helped Annabel out of the car. "Just be careful where you step. You don't want to have a fall."

"Is Mr. Langston here?" Annabel asked.

"Not now. He was here earlier."

"Oh." Annabel looked disappointed. "I wanted to ask him something. Oh well, I'll call him at his office in the morning."

The contractor pulled a piece of paper out of his jacket pocket. "I have a bill for you."

Annabel glanced at it. "I'll give it to my husband."

"I'd appreciate a check as soon as possible," he said. "I have to pay my men."

Annabel nodded. We walked up to the front door. It was painted green and had a fox's head for a knocker. We went in the entrance hall that had a circular staircase and into the living room. Workmen were finishing beams on the high ceiling and several others were working on a sunporch.

"We added the porch," Annabel said. "I'm going to put wrought-iron furniture here and we can sit here in the summer when it's hot."

The sunporch overlooked a pool built in a free form with rocks.

"We had to tear out the old pool," Annabel said. "This one is much prettier. And I'm going to have planting along the rocks, like a rock garden. Let's go upstairs and I'll show you the nursery and the other rooms."

I was beginning to see what Mother meant about the expense.

"This is his nursery," Annabel said. "Isn't it cute?"

The room was painted pale blue with circus animals prancing over the walls and red and white striped curtains like a circus tent. I noticed that Annabel referred to the coming baby as he and I remembered Baby Edgar who turned out to be Annabel. "I hope you have a boy," I said.

Annabel looked at me as if she hadn't considered the possibility of another girl. "If I don't, that's my final attempt," she said. "Besides, it's the man who determines the sex, so it won't be my fault if . . ." She paused. "But I know it's a boy."

We continued the tour of the house. The master bedroom had a fireplace and beamed ceilings and a large dressing room and bath. "It's a great house," I said.

"I'm glad you approve, but convince Mother, will you? She thinks it's a white elephant."

I wondered how much of this Mother was paying for. Bank vice-presidents didn't earn that much and I knew the income from Annabel's trust fund wouldn't pay for all these expensive renovations, since it was the same as mine.

"I hope we can be in by summer," Annabel said.

The baby was due in April. "Have you a buyer for the other house?" I asked.

"No, but that won't be a problem."

"Has Jean seen the house?"

"Oh yes, and she wants to advise me on the decorating. But she likes to do everything in that dreary blue-green Williamsburg shade and I like more cheerful colors."

I laughed. We both felt the same about Jean's taste.

✳ ✳ ✳ ✳ ✳

In April Mother wrote me that Annabel had had another girl. They named her Debra.

19

HERE IS A PHOTOGRAPH of Annabel with her three daughters, Gillian, Louise, and Debra. Annabel is wearing a simple linen dress with a double strand of pearls and the little girls are dressed in organdy with ribbons in their hair. A lovely family picture.

But all is not as it appears, for Annabel has fallen in love with someone else and is going to divorce Palmer.

The telephone ringing in the dark woke me from a sound sleep. It was Annabel.

"I had to talk to you," she said.

"Is anything wrong?" I had a sudden feeling of apprehension. "Is Mother all right?"

"She's fine." Annabel paused. "I'm getting a divorce."

"Can't you work it out?" I knew how crazy Palmer was about Annabel and the girls. "Have you been to a marriage counselor? After all, you have three children to think about."

"There's someone else."

"I see."

"You have that criticizing tone in your voice just like Mother," Annabel said.

"Have you told her?"

"Not yet. There are several problems to be worked out first."

"Like . . .?"

"He's married too. But his wife is a real shrew and it's a marriage in name only."

"Does he have any children?"

"Two little boys. But he's planning to get custody of them because his wife's so awful."

"Do I know him?"

"I don't think so. Though you may have heard me mention him. He's an architect, Hugh Langston."

The handsome architect who played polo. Now the pieces were starting to fit together.

"Actually, he's the architect who designed our house in McLean. That's how we met. We fell in love over the blueprints." Annabel giggled. "Isn't that romantic?"

"What about Palmer? Has he agreed to a divorce?"

"That's the problem. One of them. But I was never in love with Palmer. You know that. I married him on the rebound from Miguel."

"That still doesn't make it right. You're breaking up two families."

"I don't care. I love Hugh and he loves me. Should we be chained forever to two people we can't stand? Is that right?"

"Annabel, I'm not trying to pass judgement on you. But why don't you give it some time before you do anything rash?"

"It's too late."

"What do you mean?"

"That awful wife of Hugh's—Elaine—followed us one evening in her car and confronted us. She spat on me and broke my pearls and tore my dress. Then she telephoned Palmer and told him. I'm afraid there's going to be an awful scandal."

"Oh, Annabel . . ."

"If you're going to act that way, I'm sorry I told you. I thought I could at least confide in my sister."

"You can. Listen, Annabel, I'll write you a letter. I can't make sense when I'm still groggy with sleep."

I hung up the phone but I couldn't get back to sleep after Annabel's disturbing call. I tossed and turned and soon dawn crept over the Paris rooftops and I was still awake.

"I'm worried about my sister," I said to Darren the next evening over dinner at *La Coupole*. I told him about Annabel's call.

"From what I've heard of Annabel, she pretty much does what she likes and lets the chips fall where they may."

"But what can I do? I'm afraid she's headed for a terrible disaster."

"You can't do anything. It's not your problem."

"You don't sound very sympathetic."

"Annabel thinks only of herself. Some people are like that. You're not, so perhaps you can't see that side of her."

I wondered if Darren was right. Annabel was my younger sister and perhaps I had tried to protect her because of that. Had I a blind spot about Annabel?

"You've never met Annabel," I said defensively.

"No, but I'm sure I will when we get married."

"Married?" This from the man who had dropped his long-time girlfriend when she started talking about a rose-covered cottage and children? "Is this a proposal?" I asked.

"Don't you think it's about time?" He reached for my hand across the table. "Unless, of course, you're getting tired of me."

I smiled. "I'm not tired of you."

"And do you want to be with me always? Till death do us part?"

"Always." I didn't want to say the rest of it.

"This calls for champagne," Darren said.

And we drank to us and our future and all the wonderful times that lay ahead. Then he said something that sent a shiver up my spine. "I'm going to be reassigned."

"Where to?"

"I don't know yet."

But of course he couldn't stay in Paris forever, though it seemed like home to both of us now.

"I have to go back to Washington next month. You could come with me and we can get married there."

I thought of Mother trying to arrange a wedding at such short notice, and now with all the problems with Annabel. "It might be better to get married in Paris," I said.

"Whatever you'd like."

"After all, most of our friends are here."

So it was arranged. We would have a quiet wedding in Paris the following week with our closest friends, and this time I would be happy forever.

Another frantic call came from Annabel.

"Palmer wants the house in McLean and the two youngest children. He sent me a letter from his lawyer. If I don't agree, he's going to say in court that Gillian isn't his."

"Oh, no!" I felt sorry for my godchild Gillian, a thin awkward girl who wanted to be a ballerina. This was really going to be a messy case and it didn't seem like the time to tell Annabel about my coming marriage to Darren.

"He hired a detective," Annabel continued. "I went up to New York to have my hair streaked—at least that's what I told Palmer—but I met Hugh there and we stayed at the Plaza together and this detective got photographs and they showed them to Hugh's wife. Now she has a lawyer."

"How is Mother taking all this?" I asked.

"Badly. She thinks I should stay with Palmer. She says I'll be punished for this. But I don't care!"

"Annabel, I'm coming home in several weeks, so maybe I can talk to Palmer then."

"Oh, would you?"

"And I have some news of my own. But I'll tell you when I see you."

20

WE TOOK A TAXI from Dulles Airport and I dropped Darren off at the *Washington Post*.

"I'll see you later at the house, darling," I said.

That would give me a chance to break the news to Mother alone rather than walking in with Darren and saying, "This is my husband."

Darren kissed me and hurried into the *Post* building. Each time I felt like a stranger returning to Washington and as the cab driver continued up Massachusetts Avenue past the embassies I looked out the window at the trees with their gold, red and bronze leaves and thought how autumn had always been my favorite season here.

"You turn right at the next street," I told the driver.

He turned onto Tracy Place and I pointed out the house. I took a deep breath and tried to calm myself before confronting Mother. Why had I always been so frightened of her disapproval and criticism? I hoped if I ever had children they wouldn't feel that way about me and dread coming home.

"Please bring the bags in," I said. Darren's suitcases were in the trunk with mine. I went up the front steps and rang the doorbell. Lavinia answered it.

"Miss Barbara!" Her face beamed.

"Lavinia! It's so good to see you." I threw my arms around her and gave her a hug. "Where's Mother?"

"Down in the cellar talking to the furnace man. She's in the worst mood."

"Oh?"

The cab driver was standing impatiently with the bags. "Those go up to the third floor. Lavinia will show you the way." I paid him and gave him a large tip and then went into the kitchen and called down the stairs leading to the cellar, "Mother, it's Barbara. I'm home."

"Barbara! I'll be right up."

The kitchen table where I used to confide in Lavinia and help her shell peas had been recovered in a different oilcloth pattern, green and white with ivy leaves. I liked the old pattern better but I guess it was no longer available.

"Barbara." Mother came up the stairs slightly out of breath. She kissed me on the cheek. "These people make me so darn mad," she said. "Trying to overcharge me just because I'm a woman alone. The man tried to tell me I need a new furnace. I told him he can fix this one."

"Do you need a new furnace?"

"It will last for another year. Come on, let's go in the library. I want to know everything you've been doing. I'm so happy to see you. You never give me any problems. I'm at my wits end with Annabel!" Mother sighed.

There was no way I could avoid telling her my news, but this certainly wasn't a great time. I steeled myself and said, "I have something to tell you, Mother."

"I hope it's something I want to hear. I don't know if I can take any more unpleasant surprises at my age."

I took a deep breath. "I'm married."

Mother let out a gasp and I continued in a hurry. "I know

you'll like him and you kept saying that you hoped I'd find someone to make me happy and now I have."

Mother looked as if she might faint. "Who . . . who is this man?"

"His name's Darren McLeod and he's a foreign correspondent for the *Washington Post*. He's been head of their Paris bureau. That's how we met."

"Well, this certainly is a shock."

"I hope you're not too upset, Mother. I'm sure you'll like Darren when you meet him. Everyone does."

"So you're going to continue living in Paris?"

"No, he's getting a new assignment. He's at the paper now and he'll be here in an hour or two."

"I think I need a drink," Mother said. "Let's go in the bar."

We went in the bar off the kitchen that used to be the children's dining room when Annabel and I were small. Now it was painted with scenes resembling a Paris bistro.

Mother poured herself a glass of Dubonnet and I joined her.

Mother got back to the subject of Annabel. "I just don't know what to do about her. She has a nice, stable husband and three darling girls, and she wants to break up her family and another family as well. For what? A passing infatuation?"

"Is this other man going to get a divorce as well?" I try to pretend I don't know his name or anything about him to see what Mother will say.

"Annabel says he is. He's very handsome and I know that Palmer can be a bit trying at times, but no man is perfect."

I wondered if she was referring to Daddy. I still can't get used to coming home and not seeing him here.

"I'll talk to Annabel," I said.

"I wish you would. You're so much more sensible."

I'm not so sure I am but I'm glad Mother thinks so. "At least I'll try," I said. "Let me give her a call now."

"You're home," Annabel says on the phone. "I can't wait to see you. What's the news you had to tell me?"

"I'm married."

"Don't tell me, let me guess. To the journalist you were seeing, the one you said wasn't the marrying kind?"

"That's the one. Darren McLeod."

"Well I'm glad you've done something to take the heat off me. Mother's talking as if I'm a scarlet woman. Now she can concentrate on you. I bet she went into shock when you told her."

"She was a bit surprised, but she's taking it very well."

"That's good." Annabel sounded disappointed. "When do I meet him?"

"Let's all have dinner together tomorrow night."

"Fine. There's a new restaurant in Georgetown I think you'd like. It's opened since you were here last."

"Great."

"In the meantime, why don't you drive out to the house tomorrow and I'll fix us some lunch and we can have a long talk."

"Won't that be awkward?"

"You mean with Palmer? He won't be here, he'll be at the bank. And he's sleeping in another part of the house, so I hardly ever see him. I wish he'd move out, but he thinks I should. Can you imagine?"

"Sounds a bit sticky," I said.

"I think he has a lot of gall when it was mostly Mother's money that paid for this house," Annabel said. "Anyway, I'll see you tomorrow around noon."

"I'll be looking forward to it."

Mother liked Darren, as I was sure she would when she met him.

"Thank you for Barbara," he told her. "I was a confirmed bachelor until she changed my mind."

"She's a wonderful girl," Mother said. "I hope you'll be very happy."

So that hurdle was over, and like many things, it wasn't as bad as anticipated.

Now what remained was Annabel.

21

DARREN'S NEXT ASSIGNMENT was as Middle East correspondent for the *Post*, headquartered in Beirut. But the Beirut we knew, at least in the beginning, before the fighting and the car bombings started, was truly the Paris of the Middle East. We found a charming apartment with a balcony on a hill overlooking the city and it was there that I discovered I was pregnant.

At thirty-nine I had almost given up the idea of motherhood and I was thrilled, though a little worried, because I'd heard troubling stories about having your first baby so late. But Darren was happy when I told him the news, and tender and concerned and didn't want me to walk up steps and carry anything. I assured him I was perfectly healthy and wouldn't break like a delicate piece of glass. Still, it was nice being pampered.

I wrote to Mother and Annabel and they were pleased, but Mother was uneasy about the baby being born in Lebanon and also the sanitary conditions of the hospital in Beirut. I assured Mother that I had an American doctor and that the baby would be born at the American University Hospital and that everything would be fine. She was still apprehensive. "I just wish you weren't so far away," she wrote.

Darren found Beirut exciting and stimulating and he also covered breaking stories in Israel and Syria. I made friends with wives of professors teaching at American University and visited the ancient ruins of Baalbek and the birthplace of the poet Kahlil Gibran in Basharri.

Annabel wrote, "We're still having trouble with Elaine, who doesn't want to give Hugh a divorce. Why a woman would want to hang on to a man who no longer wants her, I can't imagine!"

Annabel's words would come back one day to haunt her.

Mother was concerned about the gossip Annabel and Hugh were causing. "Palmer has agreed to a divorce, but he wants the house in McLean," she wrote. "He also made Annabel sign a paper that she would pay for the children's education. Most distressing, but I guess one can't blame him under the circumstances. This whole affair has been a terrible blow to his pride, and of course, he does love Annabel. I just hope she doesn't discover later that this was a mistake. But then, you can't live your children's lives for them, you can only give them the benefit of your advice."

I could imagine the barrage of advice Annabel was getting from Mother and I felt sorry for her.

But I was far from removed from the scene, busy fixing up one room of the apartment that had good light as my studio and looking for subjects to paint. I found a young Lebanese girl, Kamila, to do my cleaning, and she was happy for the work because she came from a large family and needed the money. One day she brought her little brother Yusef.

Suddenly I saw a perfect model and I asked Yusef if he would pose for me. It was hard to get him to sit still for long so I took some snapshots and did a few quick sketches to help me. I still had my art dealer in Paris to send my paintings to.

Annabel and her problems were far away in another world.

From the beginning the doctor had planned to do a Caesarean, so I wouldn't have to worry about running to the hospital in the middle of the night.

"And you won't have labor pains," a friend said. "Lucky you."

Todd was born early in the afternoon on the sixth of May, and it seemed odd to be able to choose a date. When I held him in my arms for the first time and looked at his tiny features I could hardly believe that at last I had a baby of my own. Darren was ecstatic.

It was true I didn't have the labor pains that I had heard horror tales about, but the pains came afterward from the incision. Every four hours I was given an injection to kill the pain. I floated in and out of a drug-induced haze the ten days I was in the hospital and my doctor sent me home with a practical nurse for two weeks after that and cautioned me not to climb stairs.

Darren cabled Mother and Annabel the news and a letter came from Annabel after I got back to the apartment. "Darn you, you would have a boy. Seriously, I'm really happy about it. Congratulations!"

It was ironic that Annabel, who so desperately wanted a boy, had only girls, while I, who would have been pleased with either, had a boy.

Mother wrote how thrilled she was to have a grandson and that she couldn't wait to see him. "But it's just too bad he wasn't born in the United States," she added. I must invite her for a visit, I thought, and felt guilty because I didn't really want to. She'd rearrange the furniture and criticize everything and make me feel like an incompetent child again. And then I thought of Daddy and how happy he would have been about Todd and how unfair it was that he hadn't lived to see his grandson and I went on a crying jag. When Darren returned from work I was still crying and he didn't now what to do.

When my depression continued and I suddenly broke into tears for no reason, Darren called the doctor who told him it was a not uncommon ailment called postpartum depression and I'd get over it eventually.

After the nurse left, Kamila came every day to help me with the baby and do the cleaning and I started to paint again and slowly I returned to my old self. She also volunteered to babysit on evenings when Darren and I wanted to go out, and those nights she slept on a cot in Todd's room.

One evening at a diplomatic function I noticed a handsome Latin-looking man staring at me, and when Darren left me for a few minutes to speak to a British journalist, he came over.

"I have a feeling we have met somewhere before. Possibly in Washington? My name is Miguel Ramos and I was attached to the Chilean embassy there."

Miguel. Annabel's Miguel. Did he think I was Annabel? I didn't think we looked alike, though of course there was a certain family resemblance. "I'm Barbara McLeod," I said. "I used to live in Washington. I was Barbara Ashford then."

"You are Annabel's sister."

"That's right."

"And how is Annabel?"

"She's fine." I did not feel like filling him in on Annabel's current mess. "Just fine," I emphasized.

"I am glad to hear it."

A plump dark-haired woman was coming across the room to join us.

"I want you to meet my wife Marta," Miguel said. "Mrs. McLeod."

I held out my hand. "How do you do."

"You have been in Beirut long?" Marta asked.

"Two years. My husband is a journalist and we have a new baby."

"How nice." Marta beamed. I was not competition after all. "We have three children."

"Oh, here's my husband now. This is Darren. Darling, I'd like you to meet Miguel and Marta Ramos."

"It's a pleasure," Darren said, shaking hands.

"I met your lovely wife in Washington some years ago," Miguel said.

I could hardly wait to write Annabel that I'd run into Miguel. "You'll never guess who I saw last night at a party, still handsome, though losing his hair . . ." Then I remembered Annabel saying after Miguel abruptly broke off their affair, "Men are bastards! You know what Miguel told me? 'What a man does is like washing his hands. A woman does it and she's a whore.' I guess that's Latin morality for you." No, on second thought, I'd better not mention Miguel.

"It's been very nice seeing you both," I told them, and Darren and I moved on to circulate with other guests.

When we were lying in bed that night Darren said, "Was that Chilean diplomat an old lover? You don't have to answer."

"Jealous?" I snuggled up against him.

"A little."

"You needn't be. He was Annabel's, not mine."

"And the wife? Or was he single then?"

"You're sounding just like a reporter, darling," I laughed. "The wife was in Santiago while all this was going on. When she joined him in Washington the affair ended and Annabel married Palmer on the rebound."

"It all starts to make sense," Darren said.

But I didn't tell him about Gillian. I felt that was a confidence I shouldn't break. Unless of course it came out in court and I hoped and prayed it wouldn't.

"Finally that witch has agreed to a divorce," Annabel wrote. "But she's making it as difficult as possible for Hugh and trying to get everything she can out of him."

I had never met Elaine but I felt sorry for her. She couldn't have been as bad as Annabel painted her and Hugh must have loved her when he married her. And they had two little boys to consider. I tried to imagine how I'd feel if a few years down the line Darren asked me for a divorce to marry some other woman. It was not a pleasant feeling to contemplate. But Darren loved me and I loved him and we were going to be together forever.

22

IN LATER YEARS everyone would be able to recall what he or she was doing on that particular day in November 1963.

I had been shopping on Rue Hamra, Beirut's Via Veneto, and stopped at my usual newsstand to get a paper. In the distance I could see pictures of President Kennedy and writing in Arabic and then I saw headlines I was able to read and I gasped. KENNEDY DEAD.

The elderly Arab who usually sold me my afternoon paper bowed respectfully. "You are American lady. So sorry about your president."

"I can't believe it." I paid him for the paper and sat down at a sidewalk café to read it in a state of shock. John Kennedy had been shot in Dallas riding in an open car and his assassin had fled. Lyndon Johnson had been sworn in as the next president. It showed President Johnson taking the oath of office on the plane before returning to Washington, a tearful Jackie Kennedy in her blood-stained suit standing beside him and Mrs. Johnson.

Other people were buying newspapers and talking in a babble of different tongues and shaking their heads.

President Kennedy was dead. Camelot was over.

Strangers, we were all friends in this moment of sorrow.

Darren called to say he'd be late for dinner. "You've heard about President Kennedy?"

"Yes, it's awful. Is it a conspiracy, do you think?"

"I don't know. I'm at the Hôtel Saint-Georges with a lot of other newsmen trying to find out just what is going on. You'd better go ahead and eat because I'll probably be quite late."

The seaside terrace of the Hôtel Saint-Georges was a popular meeting place for newspaper correspondents. I told Kamila she could go on home and I ate dinner and put Todd to bed and then I listened to the BBC until Darren returned. He looked exhausted.

"Any more news?"

"All kinds of rumors," he said. "It's hard to pin them down. Some think it's a Communist plot, others that it was just a deranged gunman acting alone."

"Could Castro be behind it because of the Bay of Pigs?"

"He could be. We may never know."

I had the feeling that Darren knew more than he was telling me. "Would you like something to eat?" I asked.

"No, thanks. I had something at the hotel. I'd just like to fall into bed at this point. I have to go back to work in a few hours."

And as more bizarre events wrote themselves into the pages of history, I wondered if Darren was right and that we would never know the real answers.

"I've finally decided to sell the house and move to an apartment on Connecticut Avenue for the few months I'm in Washington," Mother wrote. "So let me know if there's anything you'd like and I can arrange to have it shipped to you." I felt a wrench at the idea of someone else living in our house, the house I'd grown up in that contained so many memories. "I'm getting to the age when I just want to simplify my life," Mother continued. "And Annabel has been so helpful. She knows a good lawyer, Walter Jennings, who can help me straighten out my financial affairs. He lives in Alexandria and is from an old Virginia family. His mother was a Culpepper."

I could see Mother was impressed by his background. But did the fact that his mother was a Culpepper make him a good lawyer? And I didn't realize that Mother's affairs needed straightening out.

"I think I should go home for a visit," I told Darren. "Mother's never seen Todd and he's almost two years old."

"That's a good idea."

"Do you think you could come with me?"

"I doubt it. There are too many stories breaking here right now. But you go ahead. If I can get away, I'll join you."

So Darren drove Todd and me to the Beirut airport.

"Just think, you're going to go on a big airplane and fly to see Grandma," Darren told Todd. "Won't that be fun?"

"I want you to come with us, Daddy."

"And you'll meet all your cousins too," Darren said.

"Why can't you come with us?" Todd insisted.

"Another time," Darren said. "Daddy has work to do here." He turned to me. "Call me as soon as you arrive at your mother's."

"I will."

I clung to Darren before we boarded and Todd wouldn't let go of his hand.

"Have a good flight," Darren said. "And Todd, you be a good boy and take care of Mommy."

Todd was trying hard not to cry. "I will, Daddy."

We waved out the window as the plane started to taxi down the runway and I felt a pang watching Darren getting smaller and smaller until we could no longer see him.

Todd was able to sleep on the plane but I wasn't, since I had to hold him on my lap the whole time, and I felt like a basket case when we finally arrived at Mother's.

Lavinia opened the front door. "My, my, so this is the little grandson. He's a mighty fine boy."

"Is that Barbara?" I heard Mother's voice.

"Now you take your time coming down those stairs, Mrs. Ashford," Lavinia said.

I looked at Lavinia. Was there something I hadn't been told?

"She had a little dizzy spell the other day and fell in the garden," Lavinia said.

"Now what are you telling my daughter?" Mother said. "I'm perfectly fine. You're making me sound like an old woman." Mother kissed me and then picked up Todd and hugged him. He promptly started to cry. "Oh dear, I'm afraid I rushed things a bit."

"He just has to get used to you, Mother. He's never seen you before."

"You look worn out," Mother said, looking me over.

"I am. It was a long flight. Two long flights. We had to change planes in Paris."

"Then why don't you lie down and take a nap until dinner's ready? I bet Todd would like one of those nice lace cookies. Lavinia has just made some."

Todd stopped crying. "Cookie?"

Lavinia beamed. "I'll go get some. And a glass of milk."

"How's Annabel?" I asked.

"Annabel." Mother shook her head. "You'll see her. She's coming for dinner."

"With Hugh?"

"No, by herself. It isn't proper for them to be seen together so soon after their divorces." Mother sighed. "There's never been a divorce in this family before. I ran into Palmer at the bank the other day and he looked just devastated. And of course the girls are too."

"I think I'll lie down now," I said. Todd seemed wide awake and even more so when Lavinia appeared with the cookies and milk. "I want to put in a call to Darren and let him know we arrived safely."

"You go right ahead, dear. Lavinia and I will watch Todd."

I climbed the stairs to my old room and took off my shoes and threw myself on the bed and before I knew it I was fast asleep.

Annabel woke me up.

"Oh, how long did I sleep? What time is it?"

"Seven. Dinner's ready. You look exhausted."

"That's what Mother said the minute I walked in."

We both laughed. "Todd's adorable," Annabel said. "I was playing with him downstairs."

I noticed that Annabel had lost a lot of weight and her face was quite drawn. "How's everything with Hugh?"

"Fine," Annabel said. "Well, not fine, because there's been a lot of gossip, but I'm sure it will die down as soon as we're married and people accept the fact."

Annabel floated along in a golden mist of expectation that everything would turn out the way she wanted, no matter how many people she hurt. "And when are you getting married?" I asked.

"In about six months."

"Girls?" Mother's voice drifted up the stairwell. "We're waiting for you."

"I guess there isn't time to change. I'll just come as I am," I said.

"You look fine. I like your suit. Paris?"

"Yes, I got it several years ago."

"I hope Hugh and I can do some traveling after we get

married," Annabel said. "As it is, we're both in a bit of a bind, because Hugh's wife left him with hardly a sou and Palmer cleaned out our mutual savings account."

"That wasn't very nice of him."

"No, he's a bastard. He's now playing country squire in that house in McLean that Mother bought. I had to borrow money from her to get this place in Middleburg that I'm living in now as well as selling some of my stock."

So Annabel ended up in Middleburg after all, even though she wasn't able to go to Foxcroft School there. This was the first I'd heard of the house. Perhaps that was one of the reasons Mother was so irritated with Annabel.

"Girls, come on!" Mother called.

"Coming."

"Now you sit here, Barbara, next to me, and Annabel on the other side," Mother said. "And we've fixed up a chair for Todd." Mother had put two velvet cushions on the chair beside me and Lavinia brought him in and I lifted him up.

"I'm not hungry," Todd announced.

"I'm afraid we had too many of those good cookies that Lavinia made, didn't we?" Mother said. "Your mommy used to like those cookies, Todd, when she was a little girl."

"I still do."

"You always had a sweet tooth," Annabel said. "I can't eat all that sugar. It makes me ill."

"You're far too thin, Annabel," Mother said.

Annabel scowled. "You've already told me that, Mother. Several times."

Lavinia came in with lamb chops with little paper frills and mashed potatoes and peas. She had prepared a small plate for Todd who promptly said that he didn't want any.

"Then you just sit there while we eat," I said. "It's delicious. Yum-yum. Don't you want just a little bite?"

"No." He pulled off his bib.

I decided not to press it.

"Mother," Annabel said, "since you've finally decided to sell this house, I do wish you'd see that man I mentioned to you who specializes in estate planning. Walter thinks he's very good."

"We'll see," Mother said.

"That means no," said Annabel.

"Not necessarily."

"It's what you used to tell us when we were children when you didn't want to do something," Annabel said.

"It just means I don't want to make a decision right at this time," said Mother.

"We'll see," Todd said.

Everyone laughed.

Todd was tucked in bed in Annabel's old room across the hall and I thought I would fall asleep as soon as I got my call through to Darren, but I was too wound up and kept tossing and turning. Finally I turned on the light and started to rummage through drawers. I found my old scrapbook with drawings that were published in the *Washington Post* and a folder with color sketches I had done as a child. In most of them the subject was Annabel. Annabel in a blue sunsuit swinging, Annabel in a pink dress sitting on an orange cushion holding a white toy cat on her lap. We were never allowed a real cat or dog because Annabel had allergies when she was small. More pictures of Annabel wearing dresses with smocking and a ribbon in her hair or a sunbonnet. The black-and-white sketch in the *Post* is titled "Little Sister."

Little sister. I thought of our conversation at dinner. Annabel seemed to be pressuring Mother about financial decisions and it bothered me. I remembered the affidavit she had drawn up several years ago. At that time I blamed Palmer. Now I wasn't so sure. I decided to have a talk with Mother the next day and find out exactly what was going on.

"Mother, just who is this Walter Jennings that Annabel seems so keen on? Where did you meet him?"

"Annabel met him at a hunt ball in Warrenton. He's perfectly charming. He sent me flowers for my birthday."

"Yes, but is he a good lawyer?"

Mother looked surprised at my questions. "I'm sure he is. After all, he's one of us. We don't want one of those other kind of lawyers. You know the type I mean."

I didn't like the sound of this and Mother's snobbery irritated me. "But what about the lawyer you had before? The one who wrote Daddy's will?"

"Oh, he's too old now. He's really quite senile, at least Annabel thinks he is and I agree. She thought it was time I made a change."

"I see." I was going to say something else but Todd came running into the room.

Mother's face lit up. "Here's my darling little boy. How would you like to go for a walk with Grandma? It's such a beautiful day. We'll go down Connecticut Avenue and look at the shops and I think there just might be a toy store on the way."

"Is Mommy coming with us?"

"Of course," I said. I knew what Mother wanted was to show off Todd to any of her friends she might run into. It was a good thing we were here for only two weeks or he'd be spoiled rotten. "I'll get his stroller," I said.

23

ANNABEL AND HUGH have finally gotten married.

"I hope they'll be happy," Mother wrote, "but I don't see how they can be. You can't build happiness on the unhappiness of others."

Annabel sent me a color snapshot of herself with Polaris, the white German shepherd Hugh gave her as a wedding present. She is sitting on the steps in front of their Middleburg house with her arm around the dog. She is wearing a blue denim skirt and a yellow Brooks Brothers polo shirt and loafers and her bare legs are very tan.

"This is our baby," she wrote about Polaris. "Isn't he beautiful?"

Several months later Polaris ran out on the highway and was killed by a truck. Annabel was devastated.

All was not going that smoothly in the marriage either. Annabel wrote that Hugh's ex-wife had dragged him into court demanding more child support and the judge took her side. And Gillian, Louise and Debra couldn't stand Hugh's sons. I wondered if Mother's prophecy was coming true.

To get away from all the turmoil, Hugh decided to go fishing in Maine with his brother. Annabel made a scene so he invited her to come along. From Maine I received a postcard with one sentence. "Fishing camps are for men!!"

The war in Vietnam is escalating. On college campuses back home there are student protests and Lyndon Johnson is being burned in effigy along with draft cards. I look at Todd playing on the floor with his toys and I am glad he is so young and that it will all be over when he is old enough to be called up.

Darren is awaiting a new assignment and I secretly hope that it will be London or Rome. Finally it comes. Vietnam.

"Why do you have to go?" I ask. "Aren't there other reporters the paper can send? Ones who don't have families?"

"Of course. But this is an important story to cover."

"We'll be separated."

"For a little while."

I say nothing. I wonder if he requested this.

"You knew when you married me that I had to be where the action is," Darren said. "It's part of my job."

Yes, I knew that, but I guess I didn't want to face it. Or did I hope that he would change after we were married?

"You'll have a chance to spend some time now with your mother and sister," Darren continued. "Get caught up."

He was looking forward to this assignment. I could see it in his face, hear it in his voice. Be careful, I cautioned myself. Don't say anything you'll regret.

"When do you have to go?"

"In three weeks. We can get everything packed up here and have it shipped to Washington for storage until I get back."

"Mother doesn't have the house anymore." It seems strange to think of Mother in an apartment on Connecticut Avenue and not in the house on Tracy Place that we grew up in, Annabel and I. "Annabel found a decorator to help me arrange my furniture and make new draperies," Mother's most recent letter said. "The apartment looks quite attractive and I think you'll like it when you see it. And of course it's much less work for Lavinia. What a faithful soul she is! I don't know how I'd manage without her."

"I didn't mean to store our things at your mother's. There are storage companies in Washington."

I feel my heart racing. I take a deep breath. He is leaving me to deal with everything while he goes off to the latest war.

"I can get some really good articles out of Vietnam," Darren says with enthusiasm. "Maybe even a book."

Or you can get killed, I think. But he's going anyway and I'll just have to accept it.

"Darling, don't look so worried." Darren puts his arms around me.

I bury my head against his shoulder so he won't see my tears. "I love you so much."

His arms tighten around me. "And I love you. It will just be a short assignment."

Darren has left for Vietnam and Todd and I are at Mother's apartment. I am exhausted after all the packing. It is October and in November we will go down to Pinehurst, where Mother stays until May.

"How do you like my little *pied-à-terre*?" Mother asks.

It is really quite a large apartment in an older building with spacious rooms and high ceilings, three bedrooms plus a maid's room for Lavinia and a full-size dining room, as well as a living room and library.

"It's very nice." I am amazed how so much of Mother's furniture from the house was able to fit in here. "What did you do with the rest of your furniture? Did you store it?"

"Annabel was able to use it at her house in Middleburg.

She needs a lot of things with all those children—her three and Hugh's two."

"Are they living there as well?"

"Most of the time. I don't know how Annabel copes."

I'll soon find out because Annabel and I are having lunch tomorrow and she'll tell me what she won't tell Mother. "Don't tell Mother" has become a family password and I often wish I had a mother in whom I could confide and who didn't always disapprove of everything. Perhaps that's normal and all mothers are like that and you can never please them. "You're damned if you do and damned if you don't," Daddy used to say about Mother. How I wish Daddy were still alive to see his grandson. He would have so enjoyed playing with Todd.

"Do you think Annabel is really happy with Hugh?" Mother asks.

"I think so, Mother. Why do you ask?"

"Just a feeling I have. I just wish she'd never left Palmer. And that Belgian woman he's married has children of her own. He'll probably leave everything he has to them, including that house in McLean that your father and I bought. The idea of that just burns me up!"

"What's she like? Have you met her?"

"Yes. Her name's Liliane. She's no beauty but she seems very nice and obviously crazy about Palmer. Of course I'm sure he married her on the rebound from Annabel."

What havoc Annabel has wreaked in so many lives. But what I did not know then was that this was only the beginning.

24

MEMORIES RETURN, like bits of colored glass scattered on the lawn with sunlight hitting them, making them look like jewels. Nothing is what it appears. Annabel with her sweet smile and treacherous heart. My sister.

We went to Pinehurst in time for Thanksgiving. I was happy that Todd would be able to run around and gather pinecones and build Indian wigwams under the deodar trees and not be cooped up in an apartment. I had always loved Pinehurst and my childhood visits there with Grandmother and Grandfather and I was glad that Grandfather left Mother the house and not Aunt Edith.

Todd has the tiny room I used to stay in papered with scenes of Bo-Peep and Humpty-Dumpty on a yellow background and just big enough to hold a small bed, chair and bureau. It is near the back stairs that lead down to the kitchen and has a folding wooden gate at the top. I am in Grandmother's room and mother moved my green metal beds with flowers painted on the headboards to Pinehurst after she sold the Washington house. On the mahogany bureau covered with a lace runner

Uncle Edgar watches me from a silver frame. Grandmother's rocking chair is still in a corner by the window and Todd loves to rock in it.

We eat out several times a week so Lavinia won't have to cook so much, either at the Pinehurst Country Club or the hotel or the Women's Exchange. The Women's Exchange is a log cabin in the pines where country women bring quilts and children's clothes they have made and the winter residents volunteer to sell them along with homemade cookies and candy. They also serve a delicious luncheon several days a week and we are going there today.

"What happened to the black mammy that was in front?" I asked Mother. The life-size black mammy with her colorful dress and kerchief holding a broom was part of my childhood memories and the Women's Exchange didn't seem the same without her.

"Someone stole her," Mother said. "There are rumors that the N.A.A.C.P. wanted them to get rid of her."

"What's a mammy?" Todd asked.

"Like Aunt Jemima on the box of pancake mix," Mother said.

Todd still looked puzzled.

"I don't think they have that picture on the box anymore," I said, as we went through the low wooden door into the log cabin.

A friend of Mother's was behind the candy and cookie counter by the entrance and Mother stopped to introduce us.

"Dorothy, I don't believe you've ever met my daughter Barbara. Mrs. Tucker."

"No, I've only met Annabel," Mrs. Tucker said. "You must be the artist. The one who's been living in Lebanon."

"That's right."

"And the mother of the grandson," she added, smiling at Todd.

Todd was eyeing the candy behind the glass case.

"This is my grandson Todd," Mother said proudly, patting him on the head.

"Can I have some candy?" Todd asked.

"After luncheon Gramma will get you some. If you eat all your lunch," Mother said.

That sounded familiar. I remembered her stories of all the starving children in China that she mentioned every time I didn't clean my plate.

We had a lunch of wonderful homemade pea soup and chicken sandwiches.

"I don't like this soup," Todd said.

"Try just a little," I pleaded.

"You want to grow up to be a big strong man like your Daddy, don't you?" said Mother.

It was the wrong thing to say. Todd's eyes filled with tears. "I want Daddy," he sobbed. "When is he coming home?"

"Soon," I said. "When we get back to the house we'll write him a nice long letter and tell him everything you've been doing."

"And we can take some snapshots of you and Mommy to send him," Mother added.

I missed Darren horribly and Mother was beginning to get on my nerves. And I felt guilty about it because she was doing everything she could for Todd and me. The other morning he had broken a small jade statue, knocked it off a table as he was running through the living room to the sunporch to see a cardinal at the bird feeder outside, and Mother had been quite upset.

"We'll have to find some children for you to play with here," Mother said.

The trouble was that Pinehurst was a resort for middle-aged and elderly golfers and not a seaside resort where families came with small children. I didn't know where we would find any playmates for Todd.

Please, Darren, come back soon, I prayed. Being with Mother was fine for a two-or three-week visit, but months on end was another story.

I called Annabel one afternoon while Mother was at the village hairdresser and Todd was taking his nap.

"I'm going crazy here," I said.

"I don't know how you're able to stay there with Mother that long," Annabel agreed. "I'd suggest you come to Middleburg for a visit but I've got my hands full with all these children. If I'd known then what I know how about what it's like to combine two families . . ." She sighed. "Anyway, it takes a lot of work."

"Are you still having trouble with Elaine?"

"Oh yes, all the time. In fact Hugh has a court date next week. She wants more money, says she can't live decently on what Hugh gives her."

I thought that it must be hard for Elaine in such a small place having to run into Hugh with Annabel, but I didn't say so. I just hoped that Annabel was happy with Hugh after paying such a high price and disrupting so many lives.

"When's Darren coming back?" Annabel asked.

"I wish I knew. Before too long, I hope."

"Well, don't let Mother get to you. Remember, it isn't forever."

The news from Vietnam was not reassuring. The war was escalating with no end in sight. It seemed we couldn't win and we couldn't pull out.

I read Darren's reports in the *Washington Post* and trembled at the constant danger he was in. "A few months" had passed and he was still there. It was the first Christmas we'd been apart and it was especially hard on Todd. January came, then February.

"Todd keeps asking when you're coming home," I wrote him.

Mother and I watched the news on television after Todd had gone to bed and the pictures were pretty horrifying from Vietnam. Darren is in the midst of all that, I thought. I had trouble sleeping and got Dr. Brady to give me a prescription for Nembutal. Finally I drifted off dreaming of Darren.

Darren's boss at the *Post* was the one who called me.

"I wanted to reach you before you heard it on the radio or saw it on television," he said. "I'm afraid I have bad news, Barbara. I'm so sorry."

I gripped the telephone receiver so hard my knuckles were white. "Darren? He's been wounded?"

There was a pause before he said, his voice sounding strained, "It's worse than that. He was in a helicopter crash along with our cameraman. They were both killed."

Still it didn't register. "Did someone see it happen? Perhaps they were captured."

"No, they recovered the bodies. Again, my deepest sympathy. Darren was one of our best."

I sat there numbly and stared out at the pines. It couldn't happen to me twice, I thought. It just wasn't fair. Then I collapsed on the bed and lay there sobbing until Mother came up the stairs.

"Oh my dear." She gathered me into her arms.

I wanted to die. If only I could die too. But It couldn't. There was Todd. I'd have to raise Todd alone now, and he probably wouldn't even remember his father when he was grown.

"At least he died doing what he loved," I sobbed. "Why do men like wars so much? He didn't have to go."

A letter from Darren arrived in the mail the following day. I could hardly bear to read it. He spoke of the great stories he was getting in Vietnam and a terrific title he had for his book. "Kiss Todd for me," he wrote. "I'll be seeing you both before long."

Annabel rushed down, but I was so sedated I don't remember seeing her. Dr. Brady, who had a reputation for over-medicating his elderly patients on the Pinehurst cocktail circuit, gave me something so strong that I slept for three days.

Lavinia kept Todd busy and baked special goodies for him. I wondered if she'd told him that his daddy had gone to the Pearly Gates and now had wings and a halo, the way she told me as a child about Uncle Edgar.

Whatever he had been told, Todd didn't really understand, because every now and then he would say, "When Daddy comes home," or "I'll show this to Daddy," when he had colored a picture in his crayon book.

"We'll have to see about a school for Todd," Mother said one day and suddenly I realized she expected Todd and me to remain in Pinehurst indefinitely. I hadn't even thought about the future. It made sense to her, of course. She was a widow and now I was one and there was plenty of room in the Pinehurst house for me and Todd. Lavinia could continue as usual doing the cooking and cleaning, and I could make Grandfather's old room into my studio.

"And you could take up golf," Mother said, who had never played herself. "Or bridge. So many of my friends play bridge. I often wish I'd learned, but perhaps it's not too late. We could take lessons together."

I didn't reply. I felt like a floppy Raggedy Ann doll that the stuffing is starting to come out of.

"Pinehurst is really a wonderful place," Mother continued happily. "Father just loved it here and I find, as I get older, that I much prefer it to Washington. A large city has so many problems. Here everyone knows everyone else and no one locks their doors. Oh, Todd, don't touch that," Mother said quickly, as Todd was about to pick up a delicate bronze figure of a dancing girl holding a glass ball.

"I only wanted to look at it, Gramma. I wasn't going to break it."

"Yes, I know, and you're a very good boy. But the dancing girl is very fragile. We have to be very careful of her," Mother said, trying to soften her earlier sharp tone. "I'll tell you what, Todd, let's go outside and gather pinecones and see which one of us can find the most. I'll give you a penny for each one you find and then you can buy some candy with your money at the Women's Exchange."

Todd brightened. "I bet I find more than you!"

"I wouldn't be surprised," Mother said. "You're a very smart boy."

I realize I'll have to pull myself together and get my own place. But where? I can't seem to think straight yet. It is so hard to imagine my future without Darren.

A few weeks later the travel section of the *New York Times* that Mother brought back from the hotel solved my problem. There was an article on Carmel, an artist's colony in Northern California not too far from San Francisco. It sounded ideal. I wanted to go somewhere that had no memories of Darren and me together. Todd and I could have one of those charming little houses that overlooked the Pacific and I was sure to find a good school for Todd. I took the travel section up to my room and read the article over several times before going to bed.

Mother would be hurt, of course, that we weren't staying on in Pinehurst the way she planned, but I had to lead my own life. Yes, this was the perfect solution.

25

THE PAGES SLIP FORWARD, years pass. Todd is nineteen and starting his junior year at Stanford. He is majoring in journalism and is editor of the college paper.

It is an afternoon in September and I am lying on my bed in my cottage in Carmel trying to take a nap after painting all morning in my studio. The lace valances above the windows are reflected on the white ceiling with their pattern of flower baskets and also the small diamond-shaped windowpanes and the geraniums in the window boxes. A breeze blows and the geraniums nod their heads. Suddenly it reminds me of the shadow figures made on the walls in my childhood, a duck, a rabbit . . .

Mood and memory mingle, nursery rhymes played on an old music box, a marionette show. Daddy made a marionette show for us and on rainy afternoons Annabel and I played together. I was the puppeteer holding the strings, Annabel the audience.

"Let me, let me," she begged, so I let her hold the marionette and she got the strings all tangled, then threw it down in a tantrum and said she wanted to play something else.

Now it is Annabel holding the strings, while I search through bank records trying to untangle Mother's estate, looking for the missing bonds, while all the time Annabel knows where they are and sits grinning like a Cheshire cat hoping I won't be able to find them.

While looking in a drawer for something else, I came across a photograph of Annabel and Hugh taken a little over ten years ago, which they sent to members of the family on Christmas. They are walking across part of their property in Middleburg with a forest of bare trees in the background. Annabel has on plaid pants and a heavy padded coat with a fur collar, her hands in her pockets and a smug smile on her face. Hugh, who is tall and lanky, wears slacks with a tweed jacket and a striped tie, his hands loose by his side, as if to say that the cold doesn't bother him and he doesn't need an overcoat. Annabel told me that he liked to sleep with the windows wide open in winter while she froze.

Annabel looks happy in the photograph, but Hugh has a perturbed expression. A year later he walked out.

It was in January of 1981, a week before Ronald Reagan's inauguration, that Annabel called me in Carmel.

"Hugh's having an affair," she said.

"Are you sure?"

"Quite." Annabel started to cry. "It's so humiliating. Everyone knew it but me."

"Who is she?"

"A blonde bimbo named Clarisse. She's from Memphis and I hear she's been married four or five times."

I tried to absorb this new information. Somehow Hugh had never seemed the type to play around. "Hugh's so different from most handsome men," Annabel once told me. "He's not at all aware of his looks. Women have always chased him but he's just interested in sports and outdoor activities."

"Where did he meet her?"

"At a horse show. She was someone's houseguest. Now I hear she's decided to stay in Middleburg and get a place of her own."

"Has Hugh asked for a divorce?"

"No, he says he doesn't want one. And he says he doesn't want to hurt me. Isn't that a laugh? He just wants to move out and think things over."

"I see."

"I wonder if Palmer suffered this much when I left him?" Annabel said, as if the thought had never occurred to her before.

"I suppose it was painful for him," I said cautiously. I didn't want to make Annabel feel worse than she already did. "He did love you."

"Well he's apparently gotten over it. He didn't waste much time remarrying."

"Does Mother know?"

"Not yet. And I want to wait as long as possible before telling her. I know only too well what she'll say. 'Why did you ever leave Palmer? You got what you deserved.' So don't say anything to her."

"She won't hear it from me." Mother had asked me in a recent telephone call how everything was between Annabel and Hugh. She always seemed to have some sixth sense when things were wrong.

"I just had to talk to someone," Annabel said. "I feel so miserable. Hugh has been rather remote lately, but I had no idea there was another woman."

I didn't know what to say to make her feel better.

"I hate him!" Annabel screamed. "How could he do this to me? And after all I did for those bratty children of his!"

There followed tearful calls over the next couple months, some in the middle of the night.

I tried to comfort Annabel, to tell her that she would get over Hugh, that time healed, it would take a long time, much longer than they told you, but she would be stronger after it, much stronger, and she could do things with her life that she hadn't done before, things she wanted to do.

"I've never known what I wanted to do. You always did."

"You'll discover a whole new person now."

"Hugh told me that he was really doing me a favor," Annabel said through tears.

"He's right," I assured her. "You'll see."

"But I've never been physically attracted to any man the way I was to Hugh. I can't live without him."

Several weeks later she made that threat real by taking an overdose of Seconal.

Thelma, her housekeeper, called me frantically. "Mrs. Langston is in the hospital," she told me. "I thought you'd want to know."

"Yes, of course," I said, alarmed. "What happened?"

"I found her unconscious last evening when I went to her room to say that dinner was ready. She had taken a whole bottle of pills. I called the rescue squad and they got her to the hospital just in time and pumped her stomach. They say she's going to be all right."

"Thank God!" I was furious at Hugh. How could he do this to my sister? "Did you call Mr. Langston?" I asked.

"Yes, ma'am. And he came to the hospital to see her. But I didn't think I ought to call Mrs. Ashford and bother her at her age. You never know what a shock it might be to her system. After all, she's ninety-one."

"You were quite right, Thelma. There's no reason for Mother to know about . . . this episode . . . at all. It would only upset her terribly."

"I think Mrs. Langston would like to see you," Thelma said.

"I'll come on right away."

On the plane ride to Washington I looked out the window at the clouds and thought about the last couple years. Mother was quite bent over and frail now, but still feisty and full of advice. She had outlived every member of her family. Aunt Edith died twenty years ago after a lengthy but with cancer and Jean ran back and forth to Winston-Salem trying to supervise various nurses whom Aunt Edith fired as soon as Jean left. It finally broke up her marriage to Bill Persky, which was what Aunt Edith wanted all along.

Mother was in Pinehurst now, still with the faithful Lavinia. She no longer had the apartment in Washington because the owner decided to turn the apartments into condominiums and Mother told me, "I'm not going to buy a condominium at my age." However moving out of the District of Columbia meant having to change her legal residency and Annabel said that Walter Jennings had suggested that Mother become a resident of Virginia. "Why Virginia?" I asked. "She's only there several weeks out of the year when she visits you on her way from Pinehurst to Lake Chautauqua for the summer. Why not North Carolina?" "Walter says taxes are lower in Virginia," Annabel replied.

Annabel was back at the house when I arrived, looking wan and pale.

"I don't want to hear of you ever doing anything stupid like that again," I said, hugging her. "I was out of my mind with worry." Had she hoped that it would bring Hugh back?

"I just got so depressed all of a sudden and I couldn't see any reason to go on living."

"You have your children and your grandchildren. And no man is worth killing himself over."

"I guess you're right." She laughed feebly. "Anyway, I botched it and I'm still here."

"If you ever get that down again, call me and I'll catch the first plane."

"I'm so glad to see you," Annabel said. "I don't know what I'd do without you." A thought occurred to her. "Mother doesn't know, does she?"

"No, Thelma didn't tell her, and I won't say anything."

That year Annabel sent me a birthday card on which she had written: "To my sister, who is also my friend."

Has she forgotten all that? Or was she so greedy that it didn't matter?

26

AFTER I RETURNED from Middleburg Annabel continued to call and I tried to comfort her and keep her cheered up.

"I'm still in love with Hugh," she sobbed. "I can't stand running into him with Clarisse. I hate him!"

"You'll get over Hugh. It just takes time. I told you that before. A lot of time."

But I had never gotten over Darren. Yes, I had gone on with my life, one has to, but the pain was still there. I knew I could never care for another man the way I had for him and though I went out on dates and had several good men friends, that was all they were, just friends. I had no desire to ever marry again.

But I had my painting and that filled my life. Annabel had no interests.

"I learned something at least from Palmer," Annabel said on the phone, sounding quite cheery for a change.

"What's that?"

"About detectives. I hired one to check up on Clarisse's

background. If she wasn't a call girl, she was the next thing to it. I mailed the detective's report to Hugh's office," Annabel said with satisfaction.

I was horrified at her vindictiveness. "But what if his secretary opens it and reads it?" I asked.

"So what? Anyway, I don't think after Hugh sees that report there will be another Mrs. Hugh Langston around here."

"What did the report say?"

"Clarisse met her first wealthy husband as a client," Annabel said. "Mother always told us men didn't marry women like that, they just took them out to have a good time but they didn't respect them. Well, to hell with respect! Clarisse is probably after Hugh's money. But what she doesn't know is that Hugh isn't rich, it's his father who is. And I don't think he's going to die any time soon, though you never can tell. When he gets a look at Clarisse, he may have a heart attack."

"What does Clarisse look like?" I was curious.

"She's tall and has long blonde hair and a very good figure. She looks somewhat like the actress in Robert Redford's new movie."

"Kim Basinger? She's gorgeous."

"I don't remember her name. I don't know anything about those movie people and I care less," Annabel said, irritated by my remark. "Anyway, Clarisse is cheap-looking. Men are such fools!"

"A fine Christmas it's going to be for Annabel," Mother told me when she called. "Hugh announced he wants a divorce to marry that woman he's been carrying on with. Can you imagine doing such a thing two weeks before Christmas?"

"Clarisse?"

"Yes, that's the one. He must be in a hurry to marry her because he let Annabel have the house without any argument.

At least she got that after losing the house in McLean to Palmer, the one that your father and I paid for."

"How's she taking it?" I asked cautiously, recalling Annabel's suicide attempt that Mother didn't know about.

"Pretty well," Mother replied. "Considering. I told Annabel that she made a mistake letting Hugh's children move into her house. She just did too much for them and Hugh always put them ahead of her."

"Well don't tell her that now. It's a difficult time for her and she's trying to hold herself together."

"And did she tell you she bought a townhouse in Washington? Can you tell me why she needs two houses? Spend, spend, spend. Just like Jean with her three places."

Now that Mother knew about the townhouse, I would no longer have to keep it a secret. "I encouraged that, Mother. Annabel wants to take some courses at Washington University during the week and get her degree."

"A college degree at her age? What would she do with it? Annabel is fifty-two."

"I think it's a good idea."

"What Annabel does need is a course in finance. She has no idea how to handle money. It just slips through her fingers."

People don't mellow as they get older, I thought, they just get more set in their ways, and Mother was certainly not getting easier to get along with.

"Let up on Annabel, Mother." I was almost tempted to tell Mother about Annabel's near flirt with death, but I had promised Annabel I wouldn't mention it to Mother and I wasn't going to now. "In Washington Annabel will be able to meet new people and start a new life for herself. Middleburg is such a small community and it's hard for her running into Hugh and Clarisse all the time."

"Then she can sell that house. Why keep such a big place now that the girls are grown and on their own?"

"She wants a country place for the weekends."

Mother sighed. "Well, all I can do is offer my advice, and if no one wants to take it . . ."

I jumped quickly into the breach. "I'm looking forward to seeing you for your birthday in Pinehurst. I'll fly to Washington and stay overnight with Annabel, then the next day we can fly down together to Raleigh. Do you still have Moses working for you?"

"Yes, he'll come pick you girls up at the airport. It will be so lovely to see you. I do hope the weather will be good then. Oh, did I tell you that Walter Jennings sent me the most beautiful arrangement of poinsettias, holly and pine branches, with little silver bells and a card saying 'To my favorite client.' Wasn't that sweet of him? He has such courtly manners, so rare nowadays."

It was the least he could do for all the money Mother was probably paying him, I thought. There was something about Walter Jennings that made me uneasy, something I couldn't put my finger on. Later, I would wish that I had paid more attention.

"Just go easy on Annabel, Mother," I said.

"I will. It's always so good to talk to you, my dear."

Todd came home from Stanford and we celebrated Christmas together. We phoned Mother on Christmas Eve. She had just returned from services at the Village Chapel.

"I'm glad you caught me," she said, "because tomorrow I'm going to the Country Club of North Carolina with Dorothy Tucker and some friends. It will give Lavinia some time off so she won't have to cook."

She spoke to Todd and asked him how he was going with his studies. "All A's so far," I heard him say.

Later he said, "Gramma's certainly got a lot of energy for someone her age."

"Yes, she's remarkable," I said.

Todd was going to spend New Year's with his girlfriend's

family in Burlingame, but I was glad to be able to see this much of him. Luckily he hadn't given me the trouble so many of my friends' children had who were involved in the drug scene. Even though I was lonely at times, I felt that overall I was very fortunate.

As the plane descended through the clouds on approach to Dulles Airport, I could see far below the Virginia countryside brushed with snow and the late afternoon sun glittering on a frozen silvery pond.

Annabel met me at the luggage carousel and I was startled by her appearance. From a few streaks in her brown hair when I last saw her, she now had so many peroxide streaks that she was almost a platinum blonde and I wondered if she was trying to look more like Clarisse.

"It's a good thing you didn't come yesterday," she said. "We had a big snowstorm. They only cleared the highway this morning."

While I waited for my suitcase she went to the parking lot to get her station wagon. "I'll meet you in front," she said. "The upper level."

"How pretty everything looks in the snow!" I exclaimed as we drove to her house.

"You wouldn't think so if you had to live in it all the time. Luckily I have four-wheel-drive on this Subaru and I'm used to driving in the snow."

"How are the girls?" I asked.

Annabel frowned. "Gillian's getting married again."

"You don't like him?"

"Let's say I think she could do better. But don't mention that to Mother."

"I won't. And Louise?" Louise had always been my favorite and she got less attention from Annabel than the other girls.

"She's working on another dead-end job. I wish she'd get

married, though marriage isn't always the answer in life, as I've found out."

I thought I'd better avoid the subject of Hugh, though I knew it was bound to come up later. "And Debra? How is she?" Debra had two adorable children and Mother had intimated in a recent letter that her marriage was in trouble.

Annabel paused. "She's fine. Though they're having a tough time financially. I wish Palmer would help out. They need a second car and I can't afford to buy them one. Palmer and Liliane are now on a Caribbean cruise, so he's certainly making plenty of money, but he won't do a thing for his own children. I guess he's still bitter about Hugh. Well, I guess he had the last laugh on that deal." Annabel laughed bitterly.

There it was. Hugh. There was no avoiding it.

"Has he married Clarisse yet?" I asked cautiously.

"Next month. I guess Elaine's having a good laugh too."

"Have you met anyone new and interesting?"

"New, yes. Interesting, no."

"I'm sure you will now that you're getting out more. I told Mother that I agreed with your buying the townhouse in Washington and that it gave you more opportunities to meet a different group of people."

"Is Mother still harping on that townhouse? God! Once you do something she disapproves of, she never lets you forget it!"

"I told her how attractive it was and what a good investment, that you could sell it later on for much more than you paid for it."

"Thanks. Maybe you can talk to her on this visit and convince her some more."

"I'll try." There were also some other things I wanted to discuss with Mother when I got a chance to be alone with her.

Moses met us at the Raleigh Airport and carried our

suitcases to the car. I noticed that he, like Lavinia, were both getting on in years and I wondered how much longer they would be able to continue working for Mother.

"You didn't get that snowstorm down here that we had in Virginia, did you Moses?" Annabel asked.

"No, ma'am."

When we walked in the Pinehurst house, Mother looked at Annabel's hair, started to say something, then, apparently remembering what I'd told her, thought better of it.

"How nice to see you girls," she said, kissing each of us.

Mother had put me in the room at the top of the stairs that used to be Aunt Edith's room, papered in morning glories and butterflies with wicker furniture, and Annabel had the bedroom papered in tiny yellow roses with twin beds pushed together with a single headboard, whose windows overlooked the pink dogwood tree when it was in bloom.

I unpacked and hung my dresses in the closet and then went down the back stairs to have a brief visit with Lavinia before dinner. I could smell a leg of lamb roasting in the oven and a lemon meringue pie was cooling on the kitchen table.

"Um, I can hardly wait for dinner," I said. "No one can match your cooking, Lavinia."

"All I do is plain country cooking, Miss Barbara, nothing special," Lavinia said, but I could see that she was pleased. "And I'll work as long as I can for your mother, but I don't know how much longer that'll be."

"That's all you can do, Lavinia." I dreaded the idea of having to get someone else to replace her. Lavinia knew Mother's habits so well and she had been faithful for so many years, but she must be close to eighty now, long past retirement age. This visit I intended to make sure that Mother had left Lavinia in her will enough to live comfortably on for the rest of her life.

"I'd better get back to Mother," I said. For some reason Mother didn't like me spending too much time with Lavinia.

Annabel and Mother were sitting in the living room in front of a blazing fire.

"That was a good picture of Todd that you sent me," Mother said. "He's certainly grown up into a fine-looking young man."

I noticed Annabel's lips curl downward. "I don't know why I couldn't have had a boy the third time round," she said. "Roll of the dice, I guess."

"But you have a grandson," I said. "Debra has that darling little boy." For a moment I couldn't remember his name. "Sean."

"Yes, he's a lot of fun," Annabel said. "And he's very bright."

"And I'm so lucky to have two such lovely daughters," Mother said. "Though I do wish we could have had better weather. I may start celebrating my birthday from now on in April when the dogwood's out."

Mother seemed to be in a very complimentary mood and I hoped it continued for the rest of our visit. Usually the visits with Mother started on a good note and then the criticism crept in and after a few days I felt like climbing the walls. But then I wondered what I would be like at ninety-two and I tried to have more patience with her. Ninety-two. I couldn't even imagine living to that age!

When Annabel went into the village the following morning, I questioned Mother about her Virginia residency.

"Walter assures me that the taxes on my estate will be lower there than in North Carolina," Mother said. "He's been giving me such good advice, which will be a great help to you girls, taxwise, when I pass on."

"Which won't be for a long time, Mother. Annabel and I will be here to help you celebrate your hundredth."

Mother waved her hand in protest. "Mercy, I hope I don't

hang around that long! But if I do make a hundred, I'm going to have the biggest celebration Pinehurst's ever seen."

"That's the spirit!"

"Anyway, Walter is having me put half my estate in bonds, Virginia bonds. That way there's no tax paid on them. Isn't that clever?"

"But suppose the IRS finds out that you spend most of your time in North Carolina and just a few weeks out of the year in Virginia. Won't that cause a problem?"

"Walter's taken care of that. Perhaps you didn't notice that I have a Virginia license plate on my car and I vote in Virginia—absentee ballot—and I've opened an account at the Middleburg Bank. Oh yes, I have a telephone in my name and I pay some of the expenses on Annabel's house like the heating bill and some other things."

"But why should you pay the heating bill for the winter on that enormous house when you're hardly ever there?"

"It helps Annabel, and Walter wants me to have some Virginia utility bills to verify my residency."

"The whole thing sounds highly illegal to me."

"I'm sure Walter wouldn't have suggested it to me if it were."

Just then we heard the front door opening.

"Oh, here's Annabel," Mother said. "Did you find what you wanted in the village?"

"Not really."

"You can take the car in to Southern Pines after lunch if you'd like while I'm having my nap. Perhaps Barbara would like to go with you."

"Fine," I said.

And so Mother's ninety-second birthday passed and then we all went our separate ways, Annabel back to Virginia, me to California.

The other day I heard from Moses that the new owners of the house in Pinehurst had cut down the beautiful pink dogwood tree that spread its blossoms under the bedroom window. I cried when he told me that. How could they? Sacrilege!

"I used to fertilize that tree," Moses said. "It just made me sick when I drove by there the other day to see what they've done to the place after I worked so hard to keep it looking nice for your mother. They've cut down other trees too. Some of those old deodars, and they've painted the house olive green."

I keep in touch with Moses to see how he's doing and if he needs anything. He said that Mother told him that she was leaving him a large bequest in her will and not to spend it all at once, but to save it for a rainy day. Well that rainy day is here. Moses is so crippled with arthritis that he can't work any more and he can really use that money.

Lavinia told me that Annabel called her and said, "Why on earth does Moses think he's in Mother's will?"

"Because your mother told him so, right in front of me in the kitchen," Lavinia replied. "She also told me I'd be a rich woman."

In the bogus will written by Walter and Annabel, Lavinia was left eight thousand dollars and Moses nothing. I hope we can right things soon and see that justice is done. And as for Walter Jennings, who engineered all this, I would like to see him go to prison for life.

27

"HUGH LANGSTON IS VERY ILL," Mother wrote me from Lake Chautauqua where she was spending August at the Athenaeum Hotel. "He has cancer and he's been given a month to live."

I know how upset Annabel must be, even though she and Hugh were divorced and he had been married to Clarisse for two years. I called her and told her how sorry I was to hear about Hugh.

"Yes," she said. "I went to see him. He'd come home from the hospital because they couldn't do anything more for him and he wanted to die at home. He had lost a lot of weight and was refusing to eat. He looked awful. Clarisse didn't want me to see him, but I'd called him in the hospital and he said he'd like to see me. I guess he felt guilty. He has a brain tumor, so perhaps that explains some of his actions. I heard he wasn't happy with Clarisse and I'm sure he regretted leaving me."

I listened with sympathy. Poor Annabel. First the humiliation of Hugh walking out on her, the way she'd done to Palmer, and then Hugh marrying what she called "this blonde bimbo from Memphis."

Hugh died in the prescribed month and Annabel and her three daughters attended the funeral. "You're the real widow," Annabel told me her friends said after the funeral. I guess she felt better to hear that.

Several weeks ago I had a dream about Hugh. We were sitting on the sofa in Grandfather's bedroom in the Pinehurst house, where Hugh had never been to my knowledge, and Annabel and her girls were downstairs ransacking the house.

"Now you see what she's really like," Hugh said.

Yes, Hugh, I see, and I'm sorry if I was short with you when you left Annabel. I understand a lot of things now that I didn't see then.

All the pieces fit together, even the missing ones that I couldn't find before.

We took Mother up on her suggestion to celebrate her birthday in April instead of on her real date in early March after the year I got caught in a terrible snowstorm and all the planes were grounded. In April the dogwood is in bloom and Pinehurst is at its most beautiful. It is hard to believe that this year Mother will be ninety-eight! Maybe she will make one hundred after all. She has already lived longer than anyone in her family.

We are also meeting in Pinehurst in April this year because Annabel is going on a six-week trip to the Orient and won't be back until then. I asked Annabel if she's told Mother about her trip yet because I didn't want to slip and say anything if she hadn't and she said she would tell Mother several days before leaving.

When the call came from Annabel at seven in the evening I didn't realize the seriousness of it, especially since her voice sounded calm and not at all upset.

"Mother's had a stroke and she's in the hospital," Annabel said, as if Mother had gone to lunch at the country club with one of her friends. "And you know I'm leaving on this trip in two weeks." Now her voice was mixed with anger and irritation.

"A stroke! How bad is it?" Mother had been having these little black-outs for several years and she would always make light of them. "Oh, how silly of me, I forgot to turn on the light in the bathroom," when she had a fall in the middle of the night, or "How careless of me to have stepped in that hole," when she passed out in the garden.

"Well she's been having these for some time, as you know, but Lavinia thought I should come down. When I see how she is I'll call you and you can decide what you want to do."

"I'll come right away. That is as soon as I can get on a plane. Unfortunately Pinehurst isn't the easiest place to get to. Why didn't Lavinia call me?"

"She called me because I'm closer geographically and can get there faster and she asked me to call you. I'm taking a morning plane so I'll be there by noon."

"What time did Mother have the stroke?" I asked.

"Around nine this morning."

It was now ten o'clock at night in the East. Annabel must have known since this morning that Mother had been taken to the hospital, but she waited over twelve hours to call me.

"Why didn't you phone me earlier?" I asked.

"I was just so busy and there were so many things to do," Annabel said.

Later I would wish that I had called Lavinia but I didn't. I made a plane reservation and arranged for a woman to stay at my house to feed and walk my dogs while I was gone and called Todd to inform him that his grandmother had had a stroke.

As it was, it took me two days to get to Pinehurst. I had to drive to Monterey to catch a plane for San Francisco, then take another plane to Atlanta where I changed to a flight to Raleigh. From Raleigh it was a two-hour limousine ride to Pinehurst.

I was surprised when Lavinia opened the front door to find that Annabel had already gone.

"When did she leave?"

"Several hours ago."

"Is Mother better?"

Lavinia shook her head. "Your sister told me she had to get back to Middleburg to take care of business. She's going on this long trip in a week."

"You mean she's going with Mother so ill?"

"That's what she said. Miss Annabel told me if there were any problems to call Mr. Jennings and he'd take care of everything. He's already arranged for her to have power of attorney so the bills can be paid."

"Power of attorney!" I gasped.

"Yes. Your sister asked me to be a witness and Doctor Brady came by and drove us to the hospital. He was the other witness. That poor lady didn't know what she was signing. She could hardly lift her arm to make what looked like a chicken scratch on the paper and the notary had to guide her hand. They told her she was signing a paper so my salary could be paid while she was sick."

I was furious with Annabel. How dare she do this behind my back? She knew only too well that Mother would never have given her sole power of attorney over her affairs. If only I could have gotten here sooner, but there was no way and Annabel knew it. A thought occurred to me. Why wasn't Walter Jennings looking out for Mother's interests? After all, that was his duty was Mother's attorney. Then suddenly I realized that he was also Annabel's attorney and friend.

"Moses says I shouldn't have signed that paper. He doesn't

trust Miss Annabel. He thinks it's shocking that she's going off on this trip."

"It wasn't your fault, Lavinia." I was sure that Lavinia had no idea of the seriousness of giving power of attorney to someone and what Annabel could do with it, transfer Mother's funds, sell her house, and I planned to put in a call to Annabel as soon as I had seen Mother at the hospital. And one tomorrow morning to Walter Jennings.

"Moses is in the kitchen," Lavinia said. "He'll drive you over to the hospital. Do you want to have dinner first?"

"No, I'll go right now."

"I'll save something for you and heat it up when you get back," Lavinia said.

It was visiting time at Moore Regional Hospital and it was difficult to find a parking space. We finally found one quite a distance away.

"I'd better go in with you, Miss Barbara, and show you where your mother is," Moses said. "It's kind of hard to find her room."

He was right. We walked down a long corridor, then took an elevator, walked down another corridor into another building and took a second elevator.

"I see what you mean," I said. "I never would have found it."

Mother was in a room by herself and her bed was next to the window looking out into the pine trees. She was lying on her back with a feeding tube in her nose and her left arm was strapped to the metal railing of her bed. She appeared to be asleep. I was shocked at her appearance, so frail and helpless, Mother who had always been so strong. "Mother, it's me, Barbara. I'm here." There was no response. I kissed her on the forehead and stroked her thinning gray hair. "I love you, Mother. I'm here." Tears blurred my eyes. Moses was standing in the doorway watching. I looked at him and then back at Mother. "Is she in a coma?"

"I don't think so, Miss Barbara. Keep trying."

The halls were noisy and nurses hurried back and forth but no one came in. On the bureau I noticed two baskets of flowers and some cards.

"Mother?" I picked up her hand, the one that wasn't strapped. It felt limp. I squeezed it trying to get a reaction. "It's Barbara, I'm here," I kept repeating.

"She was talking a little earlier," Moses said.

"Press my hand if you know it's me, Mother," I said.

Nothing.

Oh, dear God, don't let her die without knowing I'm here, I prayed silently. I knew that this was close to the end and that Mother was not going to recover.

"It's Barbara, Mother. I'm right here with you. I love you." Why wasn't a nurse with her? They shouldn't have left a woman of her age and in her condition alone this way. How could she press the nurse's bell if she needed anything? And why hadn't Annabel arranged for a private nurse?

Mother's lips started to move but I couldn't make out what she was saying. I leaned down over her.

"Yes, what is it? What do you want me to do?"

Her eyes were still closed. She tried to speak again but only a faint gargling sound came from her half-paralyzed throat. "Un . . . ugh . . . tie . . ."

"I can't understand." Did she think I was the nurse? There was still no sign that she was aware who I was.

"She wants you to untie her arm from the railing," Moses said. "It's tied to keep her from pulling out the feeding tube."

The tube was attached to a hanging bag that was dripping liquid nourishment into her body. "I can't do that, Mother," I said.

Her eyes flew open. "Untie it," she said clearly.

I smiled. That was better. For an instant there was a flash of the woman she had been, in command and used to giving orders. "It has to stay that way, Mother. I'm sorry."

"Bar . . . bar . . ." A tear rolled out of one corner of her eye as she tried to say my name.

"I'm here, Mother. Everything's going to be all right. You're going to get better and then we'll take you home." I kissed her on the cheek. It was damp and wrinkled. "You'll be walking around your garden again." Another tear. I took a piece of Kleenex from the box on the bedside table and wiped it away. "Moses is here. He drove me over. See him standing in the doorway?" I chattered on, knowing that what I was saying had not fooled her.

A nurse came in to check on her. "You must be her other daughter," she said. "The one who lives in California."

"Yes, I'm Barbara."

"She's been asking for you." The nurse took Mother's pulse, then checked the feeding tube. "You're doing just fine, Myra."

I was surprised to hear the nurse address Mother by her first name and I was sure if Mother had not been so ill she would have corrected her. "Why doesn't Mother have a private nurse with her all the time?" I asked.

"We're just following your sister's instructions. And Doctor Brady didn't think it necessary."

I was surprised that Dr. Brady was still alive, never mind practicing, and I remembered the time he treated Annabel when she fell off her tricycle. He must be in his eighties now.

"Is he on the staff here?"

"No, but he's Mrs. Ashford's personal physician. We also have Doctor Levine treating her."

"When is Doctor Levine going to be making rounds? I'd like to talk to him about Mother."

"Doctor Levine is a woman, Doctor Rachel Levine, and

she'll be back at eight in the morning. I'll leave a note that you'd like to see her."

I stayed with Mother holding her hand until visiting hours were over. Most of the time her eyes were closed, but every now and then they would open for a moment and stare at me, a watery blue, and I wondered if she had been given a sedative or if this lethargy was due to the stroke.

"I'm going back to the house now, Mother," I said, kissing her. "I'll be here in the morning. Sleep well. I love you."

There was no response.

"That old Doctor Brady doesn't know what he's doing," Moses said, as we walked to the parking lot. "He even misdiagnosed the stroke. Lavinia and I told him it was a stroke. She'd had these little ones before."

"Have you met Doctor Levine?"

"No, but I hear she's good. I don't think Doctor Brady likes her, being a woman and all. There's still a lot of prejudice in the South."

I had noticed a few odd stares as I walked along beside Moses, a black man, and I was sure that a Jewish woman doctor here wasn't having an easy time.

"It's so awful seeing Mother like this, so helpless," I said, fighting back tears.

"I know." Moses helped me into the car. "She's one special lady."

Lavinia had dinner waiting for me, roast chicken and rice and string beans.

"Oh, I don't know if I can eat anything, Lavinia." Now the tears I had been holding back came and I put my head on the kitchen table and sobbed while Lavinia put her arms around me the way she did when I was a child and upset about something.

"Now, now," she said. "You have to eat and keep up your strength. Won't do your mother no good if you collapse."

"I know. Do you have a Kleenex?"

"Here you are."

I wiped my eyes and blew my nose.

"I'll just set your dinner in the dining room," Lavinia said. "Would you like a glass of milk with it?"

"Yes, please. And I'd rather eat right here in the kitchen."

Lavinia put the plate in front of me. "I got this nice big plump chicken because I thought Miss Annabel was going to be here too. It would be a shame to waste it. And I made some lace cookies."

"Lace cookies. I haven't had those in ages."

"Well, you'll have some for dessert. If you eat everything."

I smiled. "That's what you used to say when I was little."

"You got lots to do," she said. "Can't stop eating."

Yes, I had a lot to do. And first on the agenda was to call Annabel.

"How's Mother doing?" Annabel asked.

"I was shocked at the way she looks."

"Yes, I guess we have to accept the fact that Mother's going to be an invalid from now on," Annabel said calmly.

"Invalid? She's dying!" I cried. "How can you go off cold-bloodedly on this trip?"

"Pull yourself together, Barbara. You always were over-emotional. Doctor Brady said Mother could go on this way for six months or more."

"Or she could die tomorrow?"

"Yes, that's a possibility. Look, I have to finish my packing—"

"Another thing, about that power of attorney you got—"

"Yes, someone has to be able to write checks and pay the

bills and Mother told me once that if anything happened she wanted me to have power of attorney."

I didn't believe Mother had ever said any such thing, especially in view of Annabel's spending habits. "And how will you write checks if you're in China?" I asked.

"Walter has arranged all that. The bills will go to an accountant who will pay them while I'm gone."

"I'd like Walter Jennings' home phone number."

"What on earth would you want that for? You have his office number. It's in the book."

"In case Mother dies while you're on this trip." My voice was rising to a scream. I wanted to shake Annabel until her teeth rattled.

"Very well, I'll give it to you."

I took a piece of paper from Mother's desk and wrote down the number.

"Anything else?" Annabel asked. "I really have so many things to do."

"No. Goodnight. I'll talk to you tomorrow." I slammed down the phone.

As I did so a small bottle of pills fell off the night table. I picked it up and looked at the label. Halcion. A sleeping tablet. Dr. Brady had prescribed it for Mother.

Why would a doctor give sleeping pills to a ninety-seven-year-old woman who was having blackouts? No wonder Mother was having falls when she got up at night to go to the bathroom. It was lucky that she hadn't broken a hip.

I was going to have a talk with Dr. Brady and try and get him off the case. He should have retired years ago.

In the dream Mother and Uncle Edgar are dancing a polka to music from Grandmother's music box, but they look so young that I hardly recognize them. Mother's hair is parted in the middle with long curls on either side and she is wearing a velvet dress with a wide lace collar and a sash tied with a bow in back and high-buttoned shoes. Uncle Edgar has on knickers with knee-high socks, a ruffled shirt with a jacket, and a bow tie. They laugh as they dance around the living room of the Pinehurst house and into the sunroom and out again. They are talking but I can't make out what they are saying.

Then I heard the grandfather clock by the front door with its Westminster chimes and I awoke suddenly. They were gone and it was morning.

I dressed hurriedly, putting on a blue plaid skirt and a black turtleneck. Lavinia had breakfast ready for me and Moses was at the back door ready to take me to the hospital.

"Good morning, Miss Barbara. I'll bring the car around to the front."

"Fine, Moses. I'll be with you in a minute."

I ate quickly, got my coat from the hall closet, and we were off.

The air outside was crisp and cold.

"Might be a snowstorm on the way," Moses remarked.

I looked at all the old familiar sights on the way to the hospital that were too dark to see last night when I arrived. After Mother is gone I won't be coming back to Pinehurst again and all this will be part of my past. I bit my lip trying not to cry.

Moses walked with me again to Mother's room. "I'll just see how she's doing this morning and then wait for you in the hall," he said.

The hospital was busy with doctors and nurses bustling around and trays being brought in and out of rooms. Mother had a tray in front of her and a nurse was with her. They had taken out the feeding tube.

"Hello, Mother. You're looking much better today," I said cheerfully.

Mother smiled a one-sided smile and her eyes showed that she recognized me.

"Lavinia and I are taking good care of your house for you until you come home," Moses said, and Mother's eyes filled with tears.

Just then a young woman in a white coat with a stethoscope around her neck entered the room. She was slender and attractive with dark bobbed hair and hazel eyes.

"Good morning, Doctor Levine," said the nurse.

"Well, we seem better today," Dr. Levine said. "How do you feel, Myra?"

Mother tried to say something and finally croaked out in a hoarse voice, "Fine."

"Her daughter's here all the way from California," the nurse said, and Dr. Levine glanced at me.

"I'm her elder daughter Barbara," I said, so there would be no mistaking me with Annabel. "I'd like to speak to you for a minute before you leave."

Dr. Levine took Mother's pulse, checked her chart, and then we went outside in the hall beyond earshot.

"How's Mother really doing?" I asked.

"At her age she's remarkable. When I first saw her I didn't think she'd pull through the night."

"And now?"

"It's hard to tell. All we can do is make her as comfortable as possible. Of course, the long prognosis for a stroke patient in her nineties . . ."

I knew what she was trying to tell me. Don't expect miracles. "Doctor Levine, should a woman of ninety-seven who'd been having small strokes be given sleeping pills? I found a bottle of Halcion by her bed."

"I never prescribed that."

"No, Doctor Brady did. I found the bottle at the house last night on her bedside table."

"I see." She raised one eyebrow.

"I'd like you to have full charge of Mother and not Doctor Brady. I'd like him taken off the case."

"Well, that puts me in a bit of an awkward position, but I'll look in on your mother every day and see that she gets the best of care."

"I appreciate that. Thank you, Doctor Levine."

I watched her walk briskly down the hall to her next patient and then I returned to Mother. I was right about the Halcion. From Dr. Levine's expression and what she did not say, and couldn't say against another doctor, I knew that what Dr. Brady was doing was not in Mother's best interests.

The nurse was still feeding Mother so I looked at the flowers on the bureau and read the cards. One basket was from Walter Jennings and the Get Well card was signed with a flowery flourish. Which reminded me I must call him as soon as I got back to the house.

"That's just fine, Myra," the nurse said. "You keep eating like that and we'll have you dancing out of here."

Mother smiled faintly and I sat down on the chair beside her bed and took her hand.

"How . . ." She struggled with the words. "Todd?"

"He's great, doing well at his job on the San Francisco *Chronicle*. He sends you his love."

Mother nodded, pleased.

"As soon as you're feeling better I'm going to arrange for you to be moved back to the house and be in your own room again. You'd like that, wouldn't you?"

Mother smiled.

"So you just do what they tell you and eat everything and get your strength back." I was acting like the mother now and she was the child. I wondered if I was making promises I couldn't keep, but I knew how Mother hated hospitals and I felt sure she'd recover much faster in her own home. Dr. Levine could arrange to have nurses at the house for her.

Mother had closed her eyes, as if she wanted to take a nap.

"I'm going back to the house now, Mother, but I'll come see you this afternoon."

There was no response, so I tiptoed out of the room. Moses was waiting in the hall for me.

"I just want to be sure that a nurse is with Mother before we go," I said. We went by the nurses' station and I notified them that I was leaving and would return after lunch.

"How did Mother seem to you, Moses?" I asked as we walked to the car. "Is it my imagination or is she better today?"

"Better. Seeing you has perked her up, Miss Barbara."

Good. It wasn't just wishful thinking on my part. "I have some things to do at the house, and then I'll need you to take me back to the hospital around two."

"Yes, ma'am."

"Mr. Jennings, please."

"Mr. Jennings is in conference," replied Walter Jennings' secretary. "May I take a message?"

"Just tell him that Mrs. Ashford's daughter phoned."

"Oh, just a minute, I'll ring through."

"Annabel, I'm glad you called. I've taken care of everything—"

"It's not Annabel," I interrupted. "This is Barbara. You'll be happy to know, Mr. Jennings, that Mother seems to be greatly improved."

There was a long silence at the other end of the telephone and I wondered what it was that Walter Jennings had taken care of. "I'm so glad," he said finally.

"Yes, I thought you'd be glad to hear that. And I wanted to discuss with you this power-of-attorney that you gave to my sister. Mother would never have wanted Annabel to have it. It's up to you as her attorney to protect her while she can't manage her affairs for herself."

"Annabel did suggest that the two of you have it jointly, but that could pose a problem, since both of you would have to sign every piece of paper."

"Annabel is going on a six-week trip to the Orient. How can she sign anything from there?"

"I've arranged all that. I have an accountant who will write the checks on your mother's checkbooks."

"I see." There was something about this whole arrangement that bothered me. "I still don't like it."

"Your sister has to be accountable to the court for her actions," Walter Jennings said in a syrupy voice, as if that made everything all right. He seemed anxious to get off the phone. "Just call me if I can be of any help."

I hung up the phone feeling more disturbed than ever.

"What's Walter Jennings like?" I asked Lavinia as she prepared my lunch. "Have you met him?"

"Oh, yes indeedy. He came to see your mother several times at your sister's house in Middleburg and once he drove down here to Pinehurst. Said he had to come down for a golf tournament. Something about that man I don't trust."

"Is he married?"

"He's a widower with several grown children."

"What does he look like?"

"Tall, gray hair, around sixty, I'd say."

"He didn't sound very happy when I told him that Mother was better."

"You keep your eyes open, Miss Barbara."

"I intend to."

Lavinia put my chicken sandwich and avocado and grapefruit salad on the kitchen table. "You just never know how your children are going to turn out," she said. "Like a litter of puppies, you don't know which one is going to run out on the highway and get hit by a car."

After I finished lunch I called Carmen's Florist in Southern Pines and ordered an arrangement of yellow lilies and daisies to be sent to Mother and then Moses drove me back to the hospital.

"Your mother's getting some feeling back in that left leg," the head nurse told me. "She was able to lift it for the first time. And she asked for a Coca-Cola. When I told her that wasn't allowed she said, 'Let me be the judge of that.'" The nurse laughed.

"That sounds like Mother."

"Her minister stopped by right after you left. Reverend Foley of the Village Chapel."

I went in Mother's room and saw that more flowers had arrived. On the bureau was a huge basket of red tulips from Annabel's girls and an arrangement of mixed spring flowers from her friend Dorothy Tucker.

"Your room is starting to resemble a florist's shop," I said, kissing her on the forehead.

Mother smiled and pointed to the flowers. "Lovely."

"I hear your minister came by to see you."

Mother nodded. "He . . . said . . . prayers."

"Good. They're helping. You'll be out of here in no time."

Mother looked at me. I couldn't tell whether she believed me or not. "I . . . love you . . . very much," she said.

Tears came to my eyes. It was the first time in my life that she had ever said so.

28

EVERY DAY MOTHER IMPROVED a little bit and I arranged with Dr. Levine to have her moved back to the house the following week after Annabel left on her trip. I called Annabel that evening to tell her the plans. She was horrified.

"To take Mother back to the house from the hospital would kill her. She's very happy there and she's getting good care."

"Mother is not happy in the hospital. She wants to be home and I've arranged for nurses around the clock and a hospital bed to be put on the sunporch."

"Who's going to cook for these nurses? Lavinia's too old and the strain would be too much for her."

"I've taken care of that. Moses has a cousin who can come in and cook."

"Who's going to pay for all these nurses? I have power of attorney and Walter's accountant will only pay the bills I authorize. You may find yourself out a lot of money," Annabel said.

"Don't worry about that." I was getting more furious at Annabel by the minute. "Have a nice trip."

"I'll Federal Express you my itinerary so you'll know where to reach me and Thelma has another copy at the house."

"And Walter Jennings?"

"Yes, he has one."

"Does Mother know you're going on this trip to China?" When she's so gravely ill, I thought of adding, but didn't.

There was a pause. "All I told her was that I'd be back in Pinehurst for her birthday."

"Well, as I said before, have fun on your trip."

Annabel ignored this. "But you mustn't think of bringing Mother back to the house. I discussed her condition with Doctor Brady and he suggested that if she improved she could be moved to a nursing facility at Fayetteville where they specialize in stroke patients and have physical therapy—"

"Fayetteville? That's miles from Pinehurst. Her friends and Lavinia wouldn't be able to see her. Mother would be miserable there."

"I'm just telling you what Doctor Brady said."

"To hell with Doctor Brady! Doctor Levine is a much better doctor and she thinks that Mother will be able to come home if she continues to improve."

Annabel tried another tack. "Are you planning to move to Pinehurst and supervise these nurses for several months or however long it's necessary? There are a lot of valuables in the house and when Aunt Edith was ill and Jean had nurses for her at home they stole things. Jean had to keep running back and forth to Winston-Salem and she told me later that was what broke up her marriage to Bill Persky."

"Just let me handle this, Annabel, and do what I think best for Mother." I slammed down the phone.

The following morning Annabel's China itinerary arrived by Federal Express. I read part of it to Lavinia.

"Ride a train through the fertile countryside to Hangzhou,

set on lovely West Lake, where you check in to the Shangri-la Hangzhou Hotel. The next day tour West Lake to admire its arched stone bridges leading to willow-draped isles and visit resplendent Ling Yin Monastery, tucked in the wooded hills." I looked at Lavinia. "Can you tell me how on earth I'd be able to contact Annabel if Mother should become critical?"

Lavinia shook her head. "Don't look to me like your sister wants to be contacted."

I threw down the brochure in disgust. "I'm going back to the hospital."

Somewhere I had read that a light burns brightest in the minutes before it goes out, and so it was with Mother. Just as it appeared she was getting better and I had completed all the arrangements to move her back to the house, she suddenly took a turn for the worse. Pneumonia, which had taken Grandmother, clasped its icy fingers on her. Her lungs filled with fluid, her hands and feet turned blue, her breath came in rasping gasps.

I was sitting by Mother's hospital bed when a man in a dark suit with a white clerical collar came in the room. He had white hair and a lined, kind face. "I'm Harlan Foley," he said, shaking my hand. "You must be Barbara."

"Yes."

"You look like your mother." Hastily he corrected himself. "The way your mother used to look."

A woman knows when she is getting older because then she starts to resemble her mother. My hands now have the same prominent blue veins that she hated in herself.

"I always say a prayer for Myra on each of my visits," Dr. Foley said. "Will you join me?"

I bowed my head and my eyes filled with tears and spilled over and ran down my cheeks as he prayed.

"And God bless both of you." He patted my shoulder.

"Thank you, Doctor Foley." I was afraid I was going to completely break down and start sobbing, but I controlled myself until after he had left the room.

Mother never opened her eyes.

They say that when you die you go through a long dark tunnel with light at the end where those you've loved in life are waiting to help you over. I looked at Mother. Will Daddy be there? And Grandmother and Grandfather? And Uncle Edgar? Mother's lips moved slightly as if she was trying to say something but I couldn't make out what it was. I leaned closer.

"Yes, Mother? Is there something you want?"

Her eyes flew open but it was as if she did not see me, she was looking at something beyond me in another dimension.

"Mother?"

Her eyes closed again, her breath became more labored. A nurse came in to check on her. I motioned to the nurse to come outside in the hall with me.

"How long will this go on?" I asked.

"It could be several days. It's hard to tell. I'd advise you to go home and get some sleep. We'll call you if there's any change."

So reluctantly I left. I kissed Mother and said, "Good night, sleep well. I'll see you in the morning."

That was the last time I was to see her alive. At one in the morning the hospital called me. Mother had died in her sleep without ever awakening.

Lavinia had heard the telephone ringing and came up the stairs to find me lying on the bed weeping. She gathered me in her arms the way she used to do when I was a child and tried to comfort me.

"I know, I know," she murmured. "It's hard losing your momma."

"Today's her birthday," I sobbed. "She would have been ninety-eight."

"Your mother was one grand lady. She lived a long life and now she's at peace."

"I shouldn't have left the hospital. She died all alone. I should have stayed there with her."

"Now, now, don't feel guilty and start blaming yourself. You couldn't have known when she was going to pass over."

"I was going to the hospital the first thing in the morning to wish her happy birthday." My tears started afresh. "Now I have to go back there to collect her things. They said it had to be a member of the family."

Lavinia just held me and let me cry.

"And I'll have to go to the mortuary and make arrangements to bury her . . ."

"Oh, Miss Annabel's taken care of that. She went to the Powell Funeral Home in Southern Pines before she left and paid them for the cremation."

That stopped my tears. "Annabel paid for Mother's cremation while she was still alive?"

"That's right." Lavinia shook her head in disgust. "Moses and I thought it was awful. Looks like she didn't want her to recover. And your sister spent most of her time here going through your mother's drawers and papers. She hardly spent any time at the hospital."

"I wonder what time it is now in China?" I said in a fury. I would have to call Annabel and inform her the news that she had probably been hoping for, but I was in no state to do it at present.

I didn't know if I ever wanted to speak to Annabel again. Finally I fell asleep.

In my dream I am a child again in our old house on Tracy Place. Mother is holding Annabel, my long-awaited baby sister, and the yellow stuffed giraffe is turning its long neck around in a circle as the music box inside it plays Brahms' *Lullaby*. Then, without warning, Annabel bites Mother and blood runs from her breast and seeps through her lace blouse and Mother looks surprised and screams and Daddy comes running to see what's wrong.

"She didn't mean to do it," Mother says.

Still the blood keeps coming, making a large red stain that spreads across her chest. I am afraid Mother is going to die and I start to cry.

Suddenly I woke up.

It took me a few minutes to remember where I was, and then I realized that I was in Pinehurst, today was Mother's birthday, and Mother was dead.

29

LAVINIA HAD COOKED BACON and eggs for my breakfast and when I looked at it I didn't think I could get a mouthful down, but Lavinia stood over me insisting, "You got to eat something, Miss Barbara. You're going to need every bit of strength you have."

Dear Lavinia, I thought. What would I ever do without her? I pushed the eggs around my plate and finally ate a few bitefuls with a piece of toast washed down by black coffee.

"That's better," Lavinia said. She had put the Sunday papers by my place the way she used to do for Mother.

I went up to Mother's room where the telephone was and sat down at her desk. She would never return to this room now or lie on the bed looking at the pine-papered wallpaper or feed the cardinals . . . I broke down again, and finally I pulled myself together and dialed Annabel's house in Middleburg. Her housekeeper Thelma answered.

"Mother died early this morning," I said, trying to keep my voice steady. "Do you want to get in touch with my sister?"

"I'd rather you'd call Mrs. Langston," Thelma said. "You have her itinerary, don't you?"

"Yes, I do."

"I'm sorry about your mother," Thelma said. "She was a nice lady."

"Thank you, Thelma." I bit my lip, afraid I was going to break down again. "Oh, there's another thing. Mother's lawyer should be notified. Walter Jennings. Do you want to call him?"

"Could you call him, please?"

"All right."

I looked up Walter Jennings home number in my address book and dialed it. He answered the phone.

"This is Barbara Ashford McLeod," I said. "Mother passed away early this morning."

He didn't sound surprised. Or upset. "Let me know if there's anything I can do."

"I'm going to try and reach Annabel. In the meantime, can you tell me who Mother's executor is?"

"Your mother made so many wills that I can't recall off the top of my head. I'll have to wait until I open my office safe tomorrow."

"I see. Then will you call me in Pinehurst?"

"Yes, I'll do that."

It wasn't until after I'd hung up that I suddenly realized that Walter Jennings, her lawyer and long-time friend, had never said he was sorry about Mother's death.

Next I got Annabel's travel itinerary and tried to figure out where she was. "Back through the land of fish and rice this morning to Shanghai, where you board a flight bound for Xi'an. You're accommodated at the Golden Flower Hotel, where you enjoy a spectacular Tang Dynasty dinner show this evening," the brochure read. I could try there and if I missed her the next stop was Beijing in two days. I dialed the international operator and gave her the number of the Golden Flower Hotel and Annabel's name and her tour group. There would be a delay in the call, I was informed, and they would get back to me.

It was still early on the West Coast and Todd's voice sounded sleepy when he answered at his apartment in San Francisco.

"Todd, it's Mother. I'm sorry to wake you so early but I knew you'd want to know . . ." My voice broke and I couldn't go on.

"Grams . . ." He spoke his pet name for her.

"She died at one this morning in her sleep."

"Are you holding up all right? I'll come right on."

I took a deep breath. "No, I can manage. And we can't hold the funeral services until Annabel gets back. I'll have to let you know when it is."

"You know I'm here if you need me. I'll miss Grams. She was a great lady. I love you, Mom."

"And I love you. I'll call you when I know about the services. I'm trying to reach Annabel now."

I had no sooner hung up talking to Todd than the phone rang. It was Dr. Foley. He wanted to express his condolences and ask if he could announce her death at the eleven o'clock service. He would come by the house later to see me, he said.

Moses arrived at the house and I asked him if he would drive me to the hospital to collect Mother's things. I had to get that task over sometime and now was as good as any.

It was terrible to walk in her hospital room and find it empty, a nurse stripping the bed and preparing it for the next patient. In a large plastic bag were Mother's brush and comb, her slippers and robe, and some letters and cards. The nurse handed the bag to me and I signed for it.

"Do you want to check the contents and see that everything's there?"

Tears trembled on my lashes and I had to clear my throat several times before I was able to speak. "Yes, it's all there."

Except Mother. Mother is gone and never again will I see her or hear her voice, even in disapproval, saying, "Barbara, I don't think that dress is becoming," or "Why did you do that?" There is no one anymore telling me what to do, and no one to turn to either.

I clutched the bag and walked with Moses down the long corridors in silence. I had to sign some papers in the office for Medicare and then we went to the parking lot.

In the car I opened the bag of her "last effects" and ran my fingers along the velvety surface of her aqua robe, one I had sent her for Christmas. Annabel told me that she had given Mother some thermal underwear several years ago but she had never worn it. "Annabel must think I'm an old lady," Mother told me. "I just get out and walk every day and keep the circulation going. I don't need thermal underwear." She had laughed, as if the whole idea was ridiculous. I would never hear that laugh again. I started to cry.

"Better you cry," Moses said. "I'm glad to see someone in this family with feelings. Your sister, she wasn't upset at all when she was here. Look like she been waiting for this to happen."

I have to see whether they had been able to reach Annabel. If she called while I was at the hospital, Lavinia would have given her the message. Which perhaps might be just as well. I stared out the car window in silence until Moses pulled in the driveway of the house.

Lavinia heard the car and opened the front door.

"Any calls?" I was clutching the plastic bag holding Mother's robe and toilet articles and Lavinia glanced at it and then back at me.

"Yes, your mother's friend Mrs. Tucker phoned and said she would be coming by the house. And Miss Gillian called. She said she'd call back."

My godchild, Annabel's daughter. I just wanted to lie down and not talk to anyone, but I would have to be the one to deal with everything since Annabel wasn't here. How could she have gone off to the other side of the world at a time like this?

I hung my coat in the hall closet and then went upstairs to my room. The phone was ringing in Mother's room across the hall and I ran to answer it. It was the hotel in Xi'an. The tour group Annabel was with had already left and they suggested that I try the next stop to reach my party. Finally I got the hotel in Beijing to find that Annabel had not yet arrived.

"Would you please give a message to Mrs. Annabel Langston as soon as she arrives? She's with Bailey's Pacific Tours and it's very urgent. Tell her that her mother died. She'll know where to call."

I repeated it a second time to be sure the message was clearly understood. I didn't leave my name.

The telephone woke me up at three in the morning. It was Annabel.

"I was afraid that when I said goodbye to Mother I'd never see her again. Were you there with her?"

"I'd gone back to the house several hours before. She died in her sleep."

"It's hard to believe she's gone." Annabel sniffled.

"When are you coming back?"

"Back? You have my itinerary. I return April—"

"You mean you're going to finish the tour?" I interrupted, furious.

"Well it's very difficult getting back from here. On Tuesday we fly to Wuhan and take a Yangtze River cruise. My return ticket is from Hong Kong and if I change things I'll lose my group fare and the rest of the money I've paid for hotels and everything."

I could hardly believe what I was hearing. "You mean—"

"We'll have the memorial service when I get back. I've already paid for the mortuary charges. I took care of that before I left."

"So Lavinia informed me. You were pretty sure Mother wasn't going to recover, weren't you?"

"Barbara, you're just unstrung by all of this and taking it out on me."

"Have fun on your cruise." I slammed down the receiver.

I couldn't get back to sleep after talking to Annabel and at six I went down to the kitchen to make some coffee. Lavinia heard me and opened her door.

"Miss Barbara, I wasn't expecting you up so early. I'll get dressed right away."

"No, you go back to bed. I couldn't sleep after my sister's call. Would you believe that she isn't coming back but is going to continue her trip as usual?"

Lavinia shook her head in disgust. "I'd believe it."

I squeezed some juice while the water was heating and I had put toast in the toaster when Lavinia came in the kitchen in her uniform. "You sit down and let me do that," she said.

"I didn't mean to disturb you at this hour."

"You're not disturbing me. Your mother often came down at this hour. Besides, I'm an early riser."

I drank the coffee while Lavinia made oatmeal. "I guess we'll have to wait a month to have the memorial service, so I might as well return to California in a day or so and come back later. Could you stay on until then? I'll pay you your salary."

"Whatever I can do to help, you know I'll do."

I hugged her. "I wish you could come to Carmel and work for me."

"If I were twenty years younger I would, Miss Barbara. You know I would. But I'll be eighty-two my next birthday."

This was the end of a chapter, not only Mother but Lavinia and the last of my childhood memories. All that remained of those days was Annabel.

"I don't see how my sister can act like this," I said.

"She's always been selfish, Miss Annabel has. Always thought of herself first. And she was jealous of you. I couldn't help but overhear some of the things she said to your mother on her visits. You keep your eyes open."

"Don't worry, I intend to."

I called Walter Jennings at his office in Alexandria and his secretary informed me that he was in conference. I left my name for him to call me back when he was free.

"I'll ring through," she said. "I know he wants to talk to you."

"I spoke to Annabel and she's not returning for another three weeks. Do you have Mother's will there?"

"Yes, I do." His voice was guarded. "Would you like me to mail it to you in Pinehurst?"

"No, I'll be returning to Carmel the day after tomorrow. Will you send it to me there?"

"I'd be glad to. Is there anything else I can do?"

Do whatever you're supposed to do as Mother's attorney, I felt like saying. "Who is Mother's executor?"

"There are three executors. You, Annabel, and the Jefferson Bank in Alexandria."

"I see. There's another question I wanted to ask you. How much did Mother leave Lavinia?"

"Some shares of Exxon stock."

"How much is it worth?"

"Let's see—I have some Exxon myself—around seven thousand dollars."

I was stunned. "Is that all?"

"That's what I said." His voice had an oily insincerity.

"But what can we do about that? I don't want Lavinia to know that's all she was left."

"If you and Annabel wish to give her an extra bequest, and you both agree, we can petition the court."

"I don't understand. Mother assured me only a few months ago when I was here that she had taken care of Lavinia."

"There's something else in the will," Walter Jennings said, as if he could hardly wait to tell me. "Are you sitting down?"

I was sitting at Mother's desk watching a squirrel scamper across the roof of the garage and jump onto the branch of a pine tree. "Yes," I said, wondering what bombshell he was about to drop.

"You were left five thousand dollars."

I felt as if I had been punched hard in the stomach and all the breath knocked out of me.

Hearing my stunned silence, Walter added, "I want you to know that your mother agonized a great deal over that decision. But you are getting money from your uncle's estate and Annabel is not."

I knew the amount I was getting from Uncle Edgar at Mother's death and it was nowhere near what I would have received from her estate. Besides, Mother told me that she and Daddy had given Annabel money and stock to balance what I would inherit one day from Uncle Edgar, as well as buying Annabel three houses.

Something was wrong, very wrong.

I telephoned Dr. Foley and told him that I wanted him to do the memorial service and eulogy but that I couldn't give him an exact date at the moment. "Probably in three weeks or so," I said. "As soon as Annabel returns from her trip."

He sounded surprised. "She's not coming back right away?"

"No," I said. It would not be the last time I would have to explain Annabel's odd behavior at Mother's death.

"I see."

"I want to thank you, Doctor Foley, for all the spiritual help you gave Mother. It meant a great deal to her."

"I hope it did. I was very fond of your mother. She was a grand lady, the last of her kind here."

Then I called Dorothy Tucker who also sounded surprised that Annabel was not interrupting her trip.

"Mother loved you so much," I said. "She mentioned you often in her letters to me."

"I loved Myra and I shall miss her dreadfully. It won't be the same in Pinehurst without her."

I gathered up all the cards and letters of condolence so that I could reply to them as soon as I got home.

"Hold the fort till I come back," I told Lavinia. I'd cashed some travelers checks at the bank so she could have some cash in the house and I gave it to her. "And if you need anything, call me."

"Bless you, Miss Barbara. You're sure nothing like your sister."

30

IT IS A MONTH LATER and I am back at Annabel's, having flown from California the day before.

"How much are the dogwood trees?" Annabel is saying on the phone. "I see. That's pretty expensive . . . Well, all right. I need two dozen to line my driveway . . . Can you deliver them this week? . . . But I must get them in this week or I'll have to wait until next spring."

I stand in the doorway of her bedroom and point to my watch. We should be leaving for the airport shortly to go to Mother's memorial service and she hasn't even packed.

She nods at me and continues talking to the man at the nursery. "I have to fly to North Carolina this morning," she says, "so if you'll just have the trees delivered I'll arrange to have them planted while I'm gone . . . But they must be in this week. After I get back will be too late."

Is she ever going to get off the phone? I have been packed for an hour and my suitcases are in the hall outside the guest room with my raincoat and another coat lying on top of them. After the service at the Village Chapel in Pinehurst we are flying to Pittsburgh with Mother's ashes to be buried in the Calhoun family plot alongside Grandfather and Grandmother and Uncle Edgar and Aunt Edith.

"We're going to miss the plane," I say, when Annabel finally hangs up the phone. I hate getting to airports at the last minute.

"Plenty of time," says Annabel. "I have to make just one more phone call."

I go back to the guest room. It is furnished with things that Annabel took from the house on Tracy Place after Daddy died and I almost feel as if I am back in that house. It is hard to believe that Mother is gone after such a long life. I am the one who arranged the two memorial services, the one in Pinehurst and another in Pittsburgh. I am steeling myself to get through all that has to be done and here is Annabel, not at all upset, talking about dogwood trees.

Annabel has been busy decorating this house for the past year, adding a wing over the garage and a pool and a sunporch and gold Sherle Wagner fixtures in her bath with a jacuzzi. It must have cost her a fortune and I see why Mother wondered where she got the money. I wonder too.

Annabel has finished her telephoning and calls down the hall, "Come talk to me while I pack."

She has taken several dresses out of her closet and is trying to decide which one to wear.

"This black wool needs cleaning and the shoes that go with it are at my Washington townhouse." She tosses it aside and picks up a green silk dress. "You don't have to wear black at funerals anymore." She holds it in front of her and looks at herself in the full-length mirror on the back of her closet door. "Well, perhaps it is a little bright. I'll wear my navy blue coat over it. Now, to find my navy pumps and purse."

I glance at the clock on her bedside table.

"Don't worry," she says, "it doesn't take that long to drive to Dulles."

"But—"

"Honestly, Barbara, you have a checklist like an airline pilot. You remind me of Mother!"

I sit down on the edge of the bed which is piled with unpaid bills and say nothing. I feel as if I would like to slap her.

"Just shove that junk out of the way," Annabel says. "It all accumulated while I was on my trip. I'll deal with it when I get back. You might want to look at some of the notes of condolence. They're on my desk. There's one from the National Symphony and the board of the Washington Cathedral. I haven't had a chance to do anything about them. It's amazing how much piles up in six weeks. And Lavinia says there's a lot of mail at Pinehurst from Mother's friends."

"I can reply to the letters," I say. "I've already written notes to the people who sent flowers to the hospital."

"Oh, would you?" Annabel looks relieved. "I've just got *so* much to do." She puts some lingerie in the suitcase. "I hope that man gets those dogwood trees here this week."

Back to the dogwood trees again. You'd think we were going to a party instead of burying Mother.

"At this time next year my whole driveway should be a mass of pink blossoms." Annabel looks out the window ecstatically. "Imagine!"

Was Annabel always so self-centered, or was it just that I never noticed it before?

"Now all I have to do is decide what jewelry I'm going to wear." Annabel opens a jewelry box that plays "Diamonds Are a Girl's Best Friend" and takes out a heavy gold choker and a double strand of pearls. "Oh, Jean is going to meet us in Pinehurst. She's going to drive from Winston-Salem in her station wagon." She waltzes around the room to the music. "Don't you love it? Gillian gave it to me for my birthday."

Gillian now has two divorces behind her and a child by

each husband. Lavinia tells me that she also has a serious drinking problem.

"Is Gillian coming to the services?" I ask.

"Oh yes, she'll be there. And also Louise and Debra."

"You know, there isn't another plane to Raleigh if we miss this one."

"We're not going to." Annabel closes her suitcases and locks them, then glances around the room. "I think I have everything. We're off."

We start down the stairs.

"I can't wait to show you the pictures that I took in China. They'll be ready at the camera shop when we get back. And I met the most attractive man on this trip. I just wish he didn't live in Boston."

So that was why she didn't fly home right away when I called her to tell her that Mother had died but continued her trip to the end.

We start out the door and Annabel remembers something. "I just want to run in the kitchen and tell Thelma about the man delivering the dogwood trees. Don't look so worried. We won't miss the plane!"

"We'll have to figure what to do about Lavinia," I said to Annabel when we were settled on the plane.

"Lavinia? What do you mean?"

"About seeing that she gets more money. She certainly can't live on the small amount Mother left her, and I can't understand it, because Mother assured me that she'd left Lavinia financially provided for."

"Well, you know Mother. She was still living back in Grandfather's time when they paid the help a dollar a day."

"I think we should each contribute fifty thousand and make it look as if Mother left it to her."

Annabel frowned. "I can't commit to any specific amount

right now. And besides, Walter says wills are public record and Lavinia would find out the truth."

"You do whatever you like," I said, trying not to lose my temper. "I'm going to give Lavinia a check for ten thousand now and tell her that it's part of what Mother left her and that she'll get the rest when the estate is through probate."

"Let's wait and discuss it with Walter when we see him next week at Leesburg."

"We get paid as executors, don't we?"

"I don't think so. The bank is the paid executor and we give all the bills to them and they collect Mother's assets and pay the taxes that are owed and so forth."

"Then if the bank is taking care of everything, why are we needed as executors?"

"I guess Mother wanted to have someone keep check on the bank. But I don't know why Mother named you as an executor when you live all the way out in California. It seems very inconvenient."

"I guess because I'm the eldest and she trusted me."

"Are you implying that Mother didn't trust me?"

"I didn't mean that at all, Annabel. Look, we have a lot to do, so let's try to get through this without having any arguments. It's difficult enough as it is."

"Walter says we have to get an inventory of the contents of the Pinehurst house," Annabel said. "I have the name of a man to call. And also a real estate broker so we can get the house on the market and sold as soon as possible."

The will leaves the house to Annabel and me and the furniture and everything else to be divided equally, share and share alike. It seems odd that there are no bequests to charity, since Mother was always so generous.

"If you don't want the furniture, I can donate some to the Washington Cathedral for their reception room," Annabel said. "I know they'd love it. And of course the girls could use some too. Palmer just doesn't do anything for them and they're having a hard time scraping by."

"Let's see when we get there, Annabel. We'll make a list and see who wants what."

31

"I WANT TO GET SOME JEWELRY to wear," Annabel says.

It is the day of Mother's funeral and as if in her honor the dogwood is in full bloom all over Pinehurst.

Annabel opens Mother's suitcase, the one she always kept in her bedroom closet that contained her will and financial records. I see several dark blue velvet bags and some checkbooks. And something else, a legal document with a light blue binding. Annabel ignores this and empties the velvet jewelry bags on Mother's bed.

"I've always wanted this pin!" she exclaims, holding up a pearl and diamond pin in the shape of a dogwood blossom. She pins it on her green silk dress and stands in front of the mirror on Mother's dressing table to admire it. "Perfect, just what this dress needed."

I would like the pin too as I love pearls but I don't want to have a fight now. Instead I pick up the legal document and see that it is a power of attorney executed three years ago giving me and Annabel joint power of attorney. With it is a letter from Walter Jennings saying to sign it, have it witnessed and notarized, and return it to him. But Mother has already done this, with the exception of returning it to him. Why, I wonder?

"Look what I found," I say, holding up the power of attorney. "All signed and notarized and naming both of us."

Annabel is busy trying on Mother's aquamarine necklace and bracelet and turns to look at me, feigning surprise. "If I'd known that was there, it would have saved me a lot of trouble," she says finally.

"You didn't see it when you were going through Mother's suitcase before?"

Annabel stares at me coldly. "No. I was looking for Mother's social security number and her insurance papers. And I don't know what you mean by 'going through.' I was only in the suitcase for a few minutes."

Something about this didn't sound right. Mother kept her social security card and Medicare information in her desk drawer and Annabel knew it. So what was she searching for during the several hours Lavinia heard closets being opened and drawers being slammed before Annabel went to the hospital to see Mother?

"Where on earth is Jean?" Annabel asks, looking at her watch. "You'd think that today of all days she'd be on time. It doesn't take that long to drive from Winston-Salem."

"Jean's always late. You should have told her to come yesterday."

The voices of Gillian and Debra drift up the stairs from the dining room. They are fighting over which pieces of silver they want. Louise wanders in the bedroom looking forlorn, her skirt hanging down in back.

"Does anyone have a needle and some thread? I managed to rip the hem out of my dress."

"I have a sewing kit in my suitcase. Come with me, Louise." Louise was my favorite of Annabel's girls and the one who always got the short end of the stick.

"Oh, thanks, Aunt Barbara." She turns to Annabel. "Can I have the tea cart in the dining room? It would be perfect to put plants on in my apartment."

"Plants?" Annabel says in horror.

"Let her have it. You pick out what you'd like, Louise." Before your sisters claim everything, I wanted to say but didn't. "I think plants would look lovely on it."

"No one takes anything from this house until the appraiser makes an inventory," says Annabel.

Louise and I go in my room and I am getting my sewing kit out of my suitcase when I hear the sound of a car on the gravel driveway and I look out the window and a station wagon is just pulling up. "Jean's here," I call across the hallway to Annabel.

"Finally," Annabel says.

"Hi, everyone, here I am!" Jean is coming up the stairs followed by Moses who is carrying her bags. She has gained a lot of weight since I last saw her several years ago. "Isn't that dogwood *divine*? I don't think I've ever seen Pinehurst looking prettier. Aunt Myra must have put in a special order for it, bless her heart."

There had been no love lost between Jean and Mother and Jean seems especially exuberant today. Suddenly her eyes light on Mother's aquamarines. "Aren't those *gorgeous*! I've always been partial to aquamarines."

Moses is still standing in the hallway holding Jean's heavy suitcases. "Which room shall I put these in?"

Annabel waves her hand in the direction of the room papered in yellow roses with the twin beds. "In there. Thank you, Moses." She puts the jewelry back in the velvet bags except for the dogwood pin she is wearing. "I'll lock these in the suitcase until after the funeral and then we can decide who wants what."

"Good idea," says Jean.

I wasn't aware that Jean was part of the "share and share alike" but she apparently thought she was.

"Do I have time to take a quick bath?" Jean asks. "I feel so dusty after driving."

"A very quick one," I say, glancing at Annabel, but Jean is already running the water and pouring bath salts in the tub.

"Be with you in a few minutes," she says.

The next thing we know Lavinia is hurrying up the stairs screaming and waving her hands. "There's water flowing into the pantry. It's coming right through the ceiling!"

"Oh, my God! The tub!" Annabel says. "I forgot to warn Jean that you can only fill that ancient tub up so far or it overflows." She knocks loudly on the bathroom door.

"I'm hurrying as fast as I can," Jean calls.

"The tub's overflowing!" I shout.

Jean appears with a bathtowel wrapped partly around her. "I'm so sorry. We should put a sign above the tub the way there is on the toilet tank to only turn it one way. Call a plumber and I'll pay the bill."

"This house is falling apart," says Annabel. "I just hope we can find a buyer to take it 'as is.'"

The funeral is over and we are back at the house. There weren't many people at the services since most of Mother's contemporaries who are still alive are in nursing homes, but the few who are up and around attended as well as members of the organ committee (Mother gave an organ to the church in memory of Uncle Edgar). Lavinia and Moses insisted in sitting in the rear of the church, even though I asked them to join the family in the front pew.

Now we are all sitting in the living room and Annabel has a legal pad and is making a list of who wants what so she can arrange with the packers to have things shipped. The plump woman I noticed Annabel talking to when I came out of the chapel after taking care of the minister and the sexton was the real estate lady and she is expected shortly as well as the appraiser and the plumber.

It is a strange feeling to be dividing up Mother's things and when I have told Annabel what I want I go out to the kitchen to talk to Lavinia.

"Is Mr. Jennings coming down for the reading of the will?" Lavinia asks me.

"Reading of the will?" Of course that is how she has seen it on television and I don't know how it is usually done, but Walter Jennings has given Annabel and me a copy of Mother's will. "No, I don't think so," I say. "But you will get what Mother left you when the estate is through probate."

"When will that be?"

"I guess about a year. Annabel and I have to be sworn in as executors at the courthouse in Leesburg next week."

Lavinia looks disappointed. Obviously she thought she was getting her money sooner.

"But I want to give you a check in advance from the estate to help tide you over and I know my sister does too."

"And Moses?"

"Moses?" In the will Moses has not been left anything by Mother. It seemed odd because he had worked for Mother for seventeen years.

"Your mother told Moses that she was leaving him something in her will and not to spend it all at once but to save it for a rainy day."

At this point Annabel walks in the kitchen. "What makes Moses think he is in Mother's will?" she asks Lavinia.

"Because your mother told him so," Lavinia insists. "She told him in this kitchen right in front of me several months before she had her stroke."

"Well I don't know anything about that," Annabel says. "Come, Barbara, we have a lot of things to do."

As we walk through the dining room to join the others I say, "Do you think there could be another will?"

"Of course not," Annabel snaps. "What makes you think that?"

"Because there are so many strange omissions in this one. And it seem peculiar that Mother didn't have a 'no contest' clause."

"If by omissions you mean that you didn't get half the estate, that wouldn't be fair when you're getting so much money from Uncle Edgar and I'm not."

I don't reply. But I am going to have a talk with Walter Jennings when I see him. Something is very wrong.

We almost miss the plane for Pittsburgh as Annabel didn't allow enough time for the limousine ride to the Raleigh airport, and when we check our suitcases they make us each sign a paper advising us that because we didn't check in half an hour before flight time, our bags probably won't be on the same plane.

"What do you mean?" Annabel screams at the man. She is carrying Mother's ashes in a mahogany box.

"Come on, let's hurry." I am dressed in the black wool dress I plan to wear at the graveside service, but Annabel has her dress in her suitcase and is wearing slacks and a sweater.

"But I *have* to have my suitcase!" Annabel insists.

"Then you should have told the limousine to be at the house earlier." I grab her arm and we run down several long corridors and board the plane just as they are about to close the doors. Perspiration is running down my face and I am out of breath and feeling dizzy. I am dressed for Pittsburgh weather and it is hot in Raleigh.

We fasten our seat belts and the plane takes off and bounces through a thunderstorm all the way to Pittsburgh, so we are never allowed to unfasten our seatbelts and the attendants can't serve the cold drinks, which I could certainly use. When we get to the baggage carousel I hold my breath as the luggage from our flight starts coming around, but finally I see my blue suitcase and right after it Annabel's two tan ones.

"Thank God!" Annabel says. "Now to get the rental car I reserved." She hails a porter and he follows us with the suitcases.

The graveside service at the cemetery the following day was simple and short, and Mother's ashes were laid to rest in the Calhoun family plot alongside Grandfather and Grandmother and Uncle Edgar and the two aunts I never knew who died before I was born.

"Well, that's that," Annabel said. "I'll see about ordering the tombstone and having it installed and let you know what your share is. Now, back to the airport."

32

IT POURED RAIN on the hour's drive from Annabel's house in Middleburg to the courthouse in Leesburg. Annabel drove around looking for a parking space and we finally found one at a paid meter on a side street a block away.

"You'd think they'd have somewhere for people to park at the courthouse," Annabel said, as we huddled under one umbrella crossing the street.

A tall man with gray hair holding a briefcase was waiting in front.

"There's Walter," Annabel said. "I wonder where the man from the bank is? He's supposed to meet us too."

Walter walked over as we approached.

"This is my sister Barbara," Annabel said.

"Yes, Mrs. McLeod and I have spoken on the telephone."

"Where's Mr. Percy?" Annabel asked.

"He'll be here any minute. In the meantime, let's get inside out of this rain."

Annabel brought up the subject first. "Walter, Barbara thinks there might be another will."

"Oh no, this is definitely your mother's last will," he said, almost too emphatically.

"Then possibly there are some missing codicils?" I said.

"Barbara, you're so suspicious," Annabel snapped. "Just like Mother!"

"I think I see Lyle Percy now," Walter said.

A short plumpish man was hurrying down the corridor.

"Sorry to be late," he said breathlessly.

"We just got here ourselves," Walter said. "Mrs. McLeod and Mrs. Langston, Mr. Percy. Mr. Percy is a vice-president in the trust department of the Jefferson Bank."

Lyle Percy had a weak chin and small blue eyes behind wire-rimmed glasses and puce-colored hair that was receding at the temples and looked dyed.

"Shall we go on in?" Walter said, and we followed him to the Clerk's Office of the Circuit Court of Loudoun County where we signed in. Walter took the will out of his briefcase and put it on the counter before the clerk. I noticed how messy the counter was and the office seemed in general disarray.

"Excuse the mess," the man said, noticing my look. "The clerk is sick today. I'm the deputy clerk. Please raise your right hands."

And Annabel, Lyle Percy and I swore that to the best of our knowledge this was Mother's last will and testament.

As we were going down the courthouse steps Annabel turned to Mr. Percy. "How long will it be before we get the money?"

"Anywhere from nine months to a year," he said. "Unless, of course, there's an audit."

"An audit?" The color drained from Annabel's face.

"Oh, yes, there's usually an audit with an estate of this size," Mr. Percy said.

"I'll be on my way now," Walter said. "Just send any bills

you have concerning funeral expenses to Mr. Percy and the bank will take care of them."

"I've already paid them," I said.

"Then the estate will reimburse you," Mr. Percy said. "Just send me the amounts."

"How much longer are you going to be here?" Walter asked me.

"I'm returning home the day after tomorrow. Unless there's anything else I have to do as executor?"

"No, we'll take care of everything," Mr. Percy quickly said. "And anything you have to sign, I'll send to you in California."

Annabel and I got in her car. "I just hope we can sell that house soon, because we are responsible for taxes and insurance and any repairs until then."

"Doesn't the estate pay them?"

"No, Walter said we have to, because the house is legally ours now, even though the estate is still in probate. Oh, by the way, I want to stop at the market on the way home. Thelma gave me a list of some things she needs. And I thought we'd go out for dinner tonight. How about the Red Fox Tavern?"

"Fine with me." The Red Fox Tavern was one of my favorite places to eat in Middleburg.

"I wish Todd could have come on for the funeral," Annabel said. "I haven't seen him in so long."

"He was planning to, but at the last minute the paper sent him on assignment to cover a story."

"You must be very proud of him."

"I am. He's a wonderful boy. Or man, I should say."

"I always wanted a son," Annabel said wistfully. "I hoped Hugh and I would have one, but he didn't want any more children. The way things turned out, I guess it was just as well."

"Tell me about the man you met on the trip." I didn't want to get started on the subject of Hugh.

"Thad? He's very attractive and interesting. He's the curator of the Boston Museum and he travels a lot."

"Is he divorced or a widower?"

"Neither. He's never been married. That's one thing that bothers me. I don't think he wants to be tied down. He lives in an apartment and he's never owned a house or even a dog. See what I mean?"

"Do you think he's . . . ?"

"Gay? No, I'm sure he isn't. Well, I guess you can never be completely certain these days, but he certainly likes women."

Annabel pulled into the parking lot of a supermarket. "I just have to get a few things," she said. "Why don't you wait in the car?"

The rain was coming down now harder than ever. "All right," I said.

"I won't be a minute." Annabel opened the car door and made a dash for it.

I watched her disappear and sat looking out at the rain and wondered why Annabel was so worried about an audit of the estate. And there was the power of attorney. Why had Annabel insisted on getting one naming her solely when there was a perfectly valid one in Mother's suitcase naming me and Annabel and Walter Jennings had the copy. Why was he helping Annabel and not respecting Mother's final wishes? And why should Mother's estate be filed in a Virginia courthouse when her home was in North Carolina? There were a lot of missing pieces to the puzzle and I intended to get to the bottom of it.

Two days later I returned to California. In later years I would remember the expression on Annabel's face as I said goodbye to her at Dulles Airport to board the clubmobile out to my plane. She looked like a cat licking up the final drop of cream in a bowl.

33

AS SOON AS I HAD UNPACKED and gotten myself settled I telephoned my attorney, who was a longtime friend, and told him the story.

"But your mother wasn't a Virginia resident," he said.

"They made her one."

"The more I hear of this, the less I like it. And sadly, it's a very familiar tale in families where money is concerned."

"But Annabel and I were always close. At least that's what I thought. I can't believe she's done to me what I think she has."

"Believe it."

"Can you write her and ask her to send me those powers of attorney? Then I'd have something to start with. As it is, I just have suspicions but no proof of anything."

"What you need is a lawyer back there who's on the scene, and you don't have any time to lose."

"But who? I don't know anyone."

"I'll get someone for you. In fact, I think I know just the man. Timothy O'Brien. I went to law school with him. He's a senior partner in a Washington law firm. And he can also practice in Virginia."

"Oh, thank you, Bob."

"That's all right. I'm so sorry about your mother. I'd be glad to help in any way I can. I'll give Tim O'Brien a call and tell him to get in touch with you directly."

Several days later Annabel called all excited.

"I've sold the house!" she said.

"So soon? Who bought it?" I hoped we'd sell it before we had to pay the insurance and taxes but I had no idea it would be this fast.

"A young couple. He works in the real estate office. You met the plump woman who came to the house when you were there? It's that office."

"Yes. How much is he offering?"

"Two hundred thousand."

"Is that all?"

"You're thinking of California prices where everything is inflated and houses sell for a million dollars or more. This is North Carolina and it's what several houses in the area sold for recently. And as you know, the house needs a lot of repairs and there is asbestos in the cellar. I think you should be delighted."

"Annabel, could you send me the powers of attorney you have?"

Her voice became chilly. "Whatever for? They aren't valid now that Mother's dead."

"Do you still have them?"

She hesitated. "I think they're around somewhere."

"Then would you send them to me?"

"I can't imagine what you want them for." She sounded angry. "Here I've knocked myself out getting the house sold and suddenly you attack me."

"I'm not attacking you, Annabel. And I think that's great

about the house. We could have had it on our hands for a long time."

"You can say that again. So I think we're very lucky."

I still hadn't heard from Timothy O'Brien but possibly he was busy on another case or out of town. In the meantime I decided to put in a call to Walter Jennings. There were several questions I wanted to ask him.

He was cordial but weary when he heard who was calling. "Yes, Barbara, what can I do for you?"

"Do you have copies of everything you did for Mother?"

"Yes, I have."

I told him about finding the power of attorney in Mother's suitcase naming me and Annabel and how surprised Annabel pretended to be when I showed it to her.

"Was it signed?"

"Yes. Signed, witnessed and notarized. There was a letter along with it from you asking Mother to return it to you but she kept it with her instead." When he was silent I added, "She probably kept it because you travel so much." Still no reply. "I'd like copies of both powers of attorney," I said.

"They're not valid anymore," he said quickly.

"I'd still like them."

"I'll see if I can find them."

"Also, could you look through your files again for the years from 1983 to the date of Mother's death and see if a codicil has been misfiled, something that changes the distribution?"

"We don't misfile things in this office." His tone was icy.

"It can happen sometimes with a temporary secretary," I ventured.

"I'll look," he said. "But I don't know what it is you think is missing."

Two days later I received a letter saying that he had

searched through his files and been unable to find anything. He must have sent it right after my phone call, so he couldn't have looked very hard. He also sent me copies of the two powers of attorney. Both were unsigned.

Five years ago when Annabel and I had returned to Washington after celebrating Mother's birthday with her in Pinehurst, we went out for luncheon at a new French restaurant, *Le Lion d'Or*, and afterward decided to see a movie at a theatre on Wisconsin Avenue. Snow had been predicted, but there were no signs of it, only chilly gray skies.

Before going to the movies we returned to her townhouse and I put on a red wool Norwegian jacket I'd bought on a Scandinavian cruise, rubber boots, and took a silver fox ski hood that tied under the chin.

"You'll never need that," Annabel said, looking at my outfit with amusement. "We'll be in and out of the car."

"I'd rather be prepared," I said, taking my umbrella also.

"Honestly, you're a scream! You'd think you were going to the North Pole." Annabel walked outside bareheaded in a cloth coat and leather pumps and we got in her car.

When we came out of the theatre two hours later the predicted snowstorm had arrived in full fury. Heavy snow covered all the parked cars and wet snow blew in our faces, making it difficult to see where we were going.

"Now if I can just find the car," Annabel said. She had parked on a side street a block away and all the cars looked alike.

"Here, get under my umbrella." I was happy that I hadn't listened to her earlier and discarded my fur hood and boots.

Finally we found Annabel's BMW and she took a snow scraper out of the trunk and started to clean off the windshield, but as soon as she cleared it more snow covered it. "Hop in," she said. "I wish I had the Subaru wagon now with four-wheel drive but I lent it to Gillian while her car's being repaired."

Luckily the car started and we inched our way blindly along until we came to a hill. Cars had been abandoned in the middle of the street and others were sliding out of control. One just missed hitting us.

"I'll go as far as I can," Annabel said, "but we may have to walk the rest of the way to my townhouse. It's only a few blocks." As she spoke the car skidded on a patch of ice and I held my breath and prayed silently. "That does it. We'd better leave the car here. It's too dangerous." She managed to maneuver the car fairly close to the curb and we got out.

The walk seemed longer than a few blocks through deep snowdrifts with icy flakes blowing in our faces.

"I can't wait to soak in a hot bath," Annabel said snuggling under my umbrella and shivering.

"Me too."

"I guess this kills our plans for tonight." We were hoping to go to a concert at the Kennedy Center with Yehudi Menuhin conducting.

"It can't be helped."

"I'll fix us something to eat and we can watch television," Annabel said.

The next morning Annabel had a ten o'clock appointment with her psychiatrist. She'd been going to the same woman for years and I hadn't observed any change.

"I'm sure she won't expect me today," Annabel said as we ate our breakfast. The sun was shining now but the snow was several feet deep and outside the window a cardinal sat on the branch of a snow-laden pine tree. "Well, maybe I'd better call her anyway."

Annabel went up to her bedroom while I finished breakfast and came down shortly with an annoyed expression. "Can you imagine? I called her and she said that of course she expected me. I guess I'd better go."

"How on earth will you get there?"

"I'll walk over to where we left the car and dig it out. They've probably cleared the streets by now." Annabel looked determined after the dressing down by her psychiatrist. "Can you find something to do here? I should be back in about two hours or so."

"Don't worry about me. I'm fine. I'll get caught up on some reading," I said.

I wonder what Annabel has told her psychiatrist about altering Mother's will and stealing most of the estate? Has she confessed, or has she lied to her also? Anything you tell a psychiatrist, like a priest, is confidential and can't be used against you.

Annabel and I grew up in the same house, we share memories of the same parents. She was the sister I wanted so desperately and was so thrilled when she finally arrived. All finished now. Annabel has betrayed me and she must pay for what she did.

34

TIM O'BRIEN CALLED from his Washington law office and apologized for taking so long to get back to me. "Bob Draper told me about your case," he said, "but I had to go out of town the next day and I just returned."

I filled him in on what Annabel had done along with Mother's lawyer and that I needed legal representation.

"These will cases are difficult to prove," he said. "But if you'd like, I'll be happy to see what I can do. My fee is two fifty an hour and the firm requires a retainer of five thousand dollars."

I blanched. At those rates I would soon go broke, yet I couldn't let them get away with it.

"All right," I said.

How distasteful to be involved in a legal battle now against my own sister. But what other way was there? Annabel has stolen, helped by Walter Jennings, not only what Mother left to me and Todd, but also what she left Lavinia and Moses, and they are helpless to fight for themselves. So I must do it.

Later that same day copies of the powers of attorney arrived from Annabel accompanied by an angry six-page letter. "I don't know why you want these," she wrote, "since Walter told me he'd already sent you copies and these look exactly the same to me."

No, Annabel, they aren't the same. The ones Walter sent me were unsigned. Yours have Mother's signature.

And the signature, if it could be called that, on the power of attorney they had her sign in the hospital made me cry when I saw it. It was an indecipherable scrawl.

I called Lavinia, who had agreed to stay on in the house in Pinehurst until Annabel got a moving van and arranged to have the house emptied and cleaned up for the new owner. In the meantime, I was paying her salary and had given her extra money for expenses.

"Lavinia, how was Mother able to sign that power of attorney? Her signature isn't even legible."

"She wasn't, Miss Barbara. She was asleep when your sister and the notary and I went in her room. Miss Annabel tried to wake up your mother but she wasn't able to. Then the notary shook her until she awoke."

"Did Mother realize she was giving power of attorney to Annabel?"

"No, ma'am. Miss Annabel said she needed to sign a paper so that her bills could be paid. The notary also told your mother that they wanted her to sign some papers so her bills could be paid."

"I see. Where was Doctor Brady?"

"He was the other witness. He told the notary that your mother was mentally competent to sign it."

"Lavinia, I've just hired an attorney to try to straighten out this mess and get you what Mother really left you and Moses. Would you be willing to talk to him and repeat what you've just told me?"

"I'd be glad to, Miss Barbara. I wish I'd never signed that paper. You watch out for your sister. She's one evil woman. Keep your eyes open."

"I intend to."

In my dream I am dressed as Saint Lucia in a long white dress with a red sash and on my head is a crown of green pine with lighted candles. I am taking a tray of ginger cookies and saffron buns and coffee to Mother's room and Kristin is following me to make sure I don't spill anything.

Suddenly we hear piercing screams coming from the nursery. It is Annabel.

"Excuse me, I must see what is the matter with the baby," Kristin says.

As soon as she turns her back I take a ginger cookie and stuff it in my mouth, almost upsetting the tray, but I manage somehow. Mother's room is dark and I start to sing "Santa Lucia" in a childish voice. I approach the bed and Mother's eyes are closed and in the pale flickering light from the candles she looks like a corpse. I draw closer. She *is* a corpse! I scream and drop the tray, but as I turn to run from the room one of the candles catches in the filmy lace canopy of her bed and then suddenly my hair is ablaze. Mother warned me not to wear a wreath of candles in my hair and I didn't listen to her and now it is too late.

With a start I awake and my mouth has a furry, gingery taste and I clutch my head to make sure my hair is not on fire. I get out of bed and go to the bathroom and brush my teeth and my tongue but I can't get rid of the taste.

We never heard from Kristin again after Mother fired her, and I've often wondered what happened to her. Did she return to Sweden, get married, have children of her own? If she's still alive she would be in her seventies now.

That Christmas Kristin was with us was when I got my beloved dollhouse, the happiest Christmas of my childhood.

We were a family then, so long ago . . .

Last summer in the Rijks Museum in Amsterdam I left the crowd of tourists looking for Rembrandt's *The Night Watch* and followed the arrows leading to the basement, past the Delft porcelain, and finally I found what I was looking for. The dollhouses. They had been made by a Dutch doctor as a hobby over two hundred years ago and were decorated in the style of the period.

In front of one of the dollhouses stood a French couple with a little girl of about five and the father held her up so she could see better. I shared her glee as she exclaimed in delight over the miniature furniture and reached out to touch it.

"*N'y touche pas!*" her father said sharply.

I know, I thought, you want to play with it, to rearrange the furniture, the way I used to do for hours with my dollhouse. It's no fun just looking at it. I smiled at her in sympathy.

After they moved on, I stayed there for a long time. Remembering.

Tim O'Brien sent me a copy of the letter he has written to Annabel requesting that she deliver Mother's checkbooks and all financial records to his law office within ten days so that we can examine them. Two days later I returned from the market to find a message on my answering machine from Walter Jennings' secretary to call him. I got in touch with Tim and asked him to return the call for me. I had no intention of being trapped into saying something I shouldn't to Walter Jennings.

Tim called back to report that Walter Jennings seemed startled that I had legal representation and said that he had no intention of turning over Mother's checkbooks or her financial records. He said that they would be given to Lyle Percy at the Jefferson Bank in Alexandria for safe keeping and we could go there to photocopy what we wanted.

This was not going to be as easy as I had hoped.

Tim wrote a letter to Lyle Percy, enclosing his letters to

Annabel and Walter and I thought: Wait until that banker finds out what Annabel and Walter have been up to!

But there was worse to come. Tim called me with very disturbing news.

"The banker appears to be in on it," he said.

"What? I thought the Jefferson was a reputable bank."

"It is. But there can always be one bad apple."

So now I had my sister, Mother's lawyer, who was also the lawyer for the estate, and a banker, the paid executor, all working together against me.

What chance did I have?

Poor Mother! She thought she had arranged her affairs so carefully so that there wouldn't be any trouble after her death. But she never realized that her own lawyer was a crook.

Several days later I received what looked like a letter from Annabel, but when I opened it, it was a card. A little girl was propped up in a sick bed and above the drawing was printed: *There's only one thing for a person in your condition to do* . . . I turned to the inside. *GET WELL!* The card was unsigned, but Annabel had put a sticker with her name and address on the back of the envelope.

So that was her tack. Annabel was the one who had been going to a psychiatrist for years, but now she was trying to imply that I was mentally ill and simply imagining all this. I called Tim and he laughed when I told him. "Just ignore it," he said. "She's trying to get a reaction out of you and hopes you'll call or write her. Don't. But save the card—and the envelope, because that proves she sent it."

Two weeks later another card arrived. This one had a rabbit, bear, squirrel, mouse, and bluebird grouped together in a garden all praying with eyes closed, while two yellow butterflies hovered above the flowers. *This special get-well message is coming just to say that many prayers will be with you until you're well to stay. GET WELL SOON*, it read.

It was also unsigned.

That was followed by a card showing two children huddling under an umbrella in the rain, arms around each other. Was that an attempt to remind me of the snowstorm when we walked along the icy Washington streets under my umbrella? *Sometimes love can touch where words can't reach*, was printed on the card. Annabel had added a message of her own. *As long as you are hurting, how can I not hurt, too?* Again, no signature.

"You're getting quite a collection," Tim laughed.

"What's going on back there?" I asked.

"We sent a paralegal from the office to the Jefferson Bank to photocopy the checkbooks, but Walter Jennings has taken off for Europe and given orders to Lyle Percy not to let us see them."

"But I'm an executor, as much as Annabel and the bank. What right do they have to do this?"

"They don't. I may have to get a court order."

"How do you do that?"

"I have to serve them and have the judge set a court date. But I can't do that until Walter Jennings returns."

"Do I have to be there?" I knew very little about court procedure and I was beginning to wonder how I was going to pay for all this. I'd have to sell a lot of paintings.

"No, I can handle it," Tim said. "Unless, of course, you want to be there."

"I don't." I'm afraid I would lose all control if I were to see Annabel again. When I think of what she has done, the way she treated Mother when she was dying, and then finding out that the will was forged and half the assets missing . . . "You take care of it."

"That's what I'm here for," he said. "I'll be in touch."

But Annabel has not yet given up on her campaign. Books followed. *Love is Letting Go of Fear, Teach Only Love, You Can Heal Your Life*. I tossed them aside.

She is still trying to twist things around, as if she is the innocent party and I am the mixed-up, greedy one.

In one of Mother's letters, which I was rereading the other evening, she wrote: "I feel one pays up for wrong doings. One may have to wait a long time, but they will suffer."

Will Annabel be caught and suffer for what she has done? Thus far she seems to have gotten away with it.

35

IN THIS PHOTOGRAPH of Mother that was taken out of an oval-shaped frame she looks about sixteen and slightly bored with having her picture taken, but now I am glad to have all these photographs. She has on another of those hats, this one with feathered plumes and a veil hanging down in back and her only jewelry is a locket on a thin chain. Her dress, or the little of it that shows in the picture, is high-necked with delicate embroidery and the collar of her coat is ermine with tiny ermine tails. Perhaps this is one of her church outfits?

Last night I heard her voice on the phone calling me long distance the way she used to. "Barbara, it's Mother. Is everything all right?"

She's still here, she didn't die. I started to speak and then I awoke. It was morning and I had been dreaming.

As the weeks turned into months and my legal bills mounted, I began to realize that hiring a lawyer doesn't necessarily solve things. Annabel now has a lawyer and the lawyers are having conferences and nothing is happening. I had hoped they would all fall apart when they first heard from my lawyer and it would be over. Tim says to be patient, that these things take a long time. And besides, he adds, we really don't have any solid proof.

"But look at what they've done. They're all guilty as hell!" I scream, suddenly feeling myself losing control.

"We have to be able to prove it in court," he replies calmly. "And all we have now is suspicious behavior on their part. I wouldn't want to go into court yet with the little evidence we have."

I wonder if I can trust any lawyer. Is he trying to string out the case so he can get more money? Mother trusted Walter Jennings and look what he did to her.

Meanwhile I am getting copies of letters Tim has written to companies in which Mother had stock, letters to banks and brokerage offices trying to trace missing bonds, and their replies, none of which yield anything we can use. The checkbooks have been edited by Walter Jennings, so they reveal nothing unusual, and it is all very frustrating. Tim has written letters to the IRS requesting copies of Mother's tax returns for the last five years and he has an accountant, a very expensive one, checking the figures. Annabel keeps insisting that this is Mother's real will, that Mother gave away most of her money during her lifetime, and that I am crazy. I am beginning to wonder. But there is a trail, if we can only pull the right thread and unravel everything.

I am having frequent migraine headaches, alternating with stomach pains. Is all this worth what it is doing to my health? Maybe I should just forget it. I certainly can't continue to pay these legal bills indefinitely. But what about Todd's inheritance that Annabel has stolen? And Moses and Lavinia, who are counting on me to recover the money Mother left them in her real will.

I take another Fioricet and put an ice pack on my head. My rage at Annabel is interfering with my creative work as well and I can't let her do that to me. I'll try to nap for a few hours and then get back to my studio and paint.

I close my eyes. A bee is buzzing outside the screen and it sounds like a chain saw. If only Darren were here to help me, he would know what to do. I need him so. Why did he have to die when we were so happy together? I try to imagine him holding me again, his arms tight around me. Can the memory of love keep you warm for a whole lifetime of loneliness? Some women can go from man to man, just to have a warm body next to them, they don't have to be in love with him the way I do. Are they better off I wonder? Not that it matters, because I can't change the way I am.

The Fioricet is starting to take over now, the blue pill of oblivion, as I drift off . . .

I was awakened by the telephone ringing, and as I reached for it sleepily in the dark, I knocked over the glass of water beside it on my night table. "Hello?"

"I'd like to know why the hell you're stirring up all this trouble," the angry voice said. It was Annabel, and at two in the morning in California, it must be five in Virginia. "And what do you mean telling the government that assets are missing from the estate? Are you accusing me of taking them?"

"Annabel, you'd better discuss this with my attorney. You have his number."

"This whole thing is ridiculous, us talking through lawyers. I'm your sister. And I can't understand why you don't think that wasn't Mother's real will. It *is* her will, and if you don't believe *me*, why don't you ask Walter."

"I have nothing to say to you, Annabel." I slammed down the receiver. Now I was wide awake and furious. My head started to throb again. I went into the bathroom and got two towels and mopped up the spilled water and picked up the broken glass. How long ago was it that I took the last Fioricet? You weren't supposed to take them closer than six hours apart and I couldn't remember. I know I took one in the afternoon, but did I take another before bedtime? I'd woken up, had some soup, let the dogs out, and then gone back to bed. I'd better wait to be safe. Am I losing my memory? I wonder. How dare Annabel suggest that I was the one who was stirring up trouble! But that was just like her. She had never admitted wrong-doing in her life.

I walked to the kitchen, the dogs following me, and poured myself a glass of milk and opened a box of graham crackers. They sat begging at my feet as I ate and I gave each of them a piece. Then I fixed another ice pack for my head and went back to bed.

But I couldn't get back to sleep. Thank you, Annabel.

I listened to the dogs snoring softly on the hooked rug beside my bed and finally I heard the chirping of birds as dawn crept across the sky.

"Mr. O'Brien is going to be in court all morning," his secretary said.

"It's urgent that I speak to him as soon as possible."

"I'll give him your message when he returns to the office."

"Thank you."

I went to my studio and tried to paint. Usually when I was painting I was able to forget everything else and become absorbed in the colors and the texture of what I was creating, but this morning I kept waiting for Tim's call, mentally adding the three hours later it would be in Washington. Finally at noon he returned my call.

Sorry I couldn't get back to you before this," he said. "But there were some complications and I was in court longer than I expected. So, what's up?"

"Annabel called me. At two in the morning."

"What did she want?"

"I think she wanted to get me off guard by calling at that hour and waking me up. She accused me of causing trouble and insisted that this was Mother's real will. I told her to get in touch with you and hung up."

"Good. The less you speak to her the better. If she calls again, just refer her to me."

That was easy for him to say. He wasn't emotionally involved. "I'd really like to say a few things to Annabel," I said. "To tell her how I always defended her when Mother was complaining about her spending, how I tried to comfort and help her when Hugh left her and she was suicidal, how I was always there for her. And then she could do what she did to me, her sister!"

"That's exactly what you shouldn't do. And remember, we still have to get solid evidence."

Spoken like a lawyer, I thought. "Has anything turned up?"

"Not yet, but I'll keep you informed."

It suddenly occurs to me that Annabel has never sent me a check for my half of the furniture in the Pinehurst house. We agreed to donate the yellow brocade sofa in the living room to the Washington Cathedral and the rest of the antiques and paintings Annabel said she could get a better price for in Virginia. I gave Annabel a check for the shipping company to crate the few items I wanted: the wisteria painting, a set of Lenox china with pine branches and pinecones on it that reminded me of Pinehurst, a small marble statue of a little girl that was by the fireplace on the sunporch, a De Haven watercolor of the woods, and a photograph of Mother in a silver frame.

I wrote Mr. Percy at the bank and asked him to get in touch with Annabel about the furniture, since she would have surely sold it by this time, and I got a letter back that he had talked to Annabel and she said that I had taken the things I wanted and everything else was on loan to the Washington Cathedral. Something about that didn't sound quite right. I thought you donated something to charity so you could get a tax write-off.

The woman at the cathedral was very gracious when I mentioned Mother's name, one of their big donors, and I asked her about the furniture that my sister had "on loan." She seemed puzzled.

"On loan? I don't know of anything on loan. We have a sofa, which was donated. And of course, we're very pleased to have it," she added quickly.

Another of Annabel's lies. Obviously she had sold the antiques and paintings and no doubt gotten a pretty penny for them. And how could I prove anything?

"The gimme gal," as Daddy called her. He knew Annabel far better than I did.

36

A FRIEND FROM WASHINGTON who had run into Annabel lunching at the Sulgrave Club wrote me that she appeared to have had a recent face-lift. A bad one, pulled too tight, so that it was obvious, and that her hair was now short and dyed platinum blonde. Was this new persona an attempt to attract another husband? I wondered. Annabel had never been very good at remaining alone without a man.

Annabel's face-lift made me recall a musical evening at a friend of Mother's when I was seventeen. The hostess was a failed opera singer and she had prepared a program of lieder with several operatic arias thrown in. As I squirmed on the uncomfortable gilt chairs beside Daddy, my attention was drawn to a woman seated across the aisle from us, a woman "*d'un certain age*" as the French politely apply to women of an indeterminate age around fifty or sixty. This lady had also had a face-lift, drawn tight like a mask under her dyed blonde hair, and I thought if she smiled broadly or laughed the face would crack. The hostess missed a high note with a screeching sound and Daddy shuddered while Mother looked daggers at him. To keep from laughing, I looked again with fascination at the lady with the face-lift and then her eyes caught mine and she saw that I was staring at her. I quickly looked down at the program in my lap, as polite applause greeted the end of the aria.

Does Annabel look like that? I wondered.

Annabel is younger than I am, but the thought of having a face-lift has never occurred to me. I've heard too many horror stories of things gone wrong, infections, one side of the face crooked, and then there was the memory of the lady with the mask. Thank you, no, I'd rather keep my own face, imperfect as it is, with small lines creeping here and there.

But that was interesting news anyway. Annabel can change her face, but she can't hide what is inside, and what is on the inside is not a very pretty picture.

Last night I dreamt of Annabel again.

I am in my room putting on make-up before going out for a dinner date when suddenly Annabel appears followed by a child of about eight or nine who looks exactly like her.

"What are you doing in my house?" I ask angrily. Did I forget to lock the door? And why aren't the dogs barking?

"I thought we could have a talk," Annabel says sweetly.

"I've nothing to say to you." I outline my mouth with a raspberry lip pencil and fill it in with matching gloss. "Except this. How can you live with yourself?"

Annabel looks startled. "What do you mean?"

"You know what I'm referring to."

"No, I don't." Her face reflected in the mirror looks innocent.

"Then I'll repeat it. How can you live with yourself, Annabel?"

"I still don't know what you're talking about."

The child is watching us both with a puzzled expression. I notice again how much she resembles Annabel. She looks just as Annabel looked at the same age.

"What is your name?" I ask the child.

"Annabel."

Of course. But how could Annabel have another child at her age? She had a hysterectomy at forty-seven.

"Everyone remarks how much alike we are," Annabel says.

"Well now I must ask you both to leave. I'm busy, and I'm going out shortly."

They make no attempt to move.

"Please leave!" I shout. "Now!"

The dream puzzled me. Was Annabel trying to appeal to my memories of her as a child in the house on Tracy Place that we both shared? Or is it a warning that I must be on my guard against her? I remember the tantrums she had as a child to get Daddy's attention, the suicide scene she staged in an attempt to get Hugh back after he left her for Clarisse. Annabel was capable of anything and she had absolutely no conscience.

Tim called me later. "Good news," he said. "At least I think it could turn out to be. Some bonds have turned up."

"Of Mother's?"

"Yes, and your sister has signed them."

"Really?" I thought of telling him about my dream of Annabel but then decided not to. "Ones that aren't listed in the estate accounting."

"It appears so."

"Then that's the proof we need?"

"Not quite. Annabel could say that your mother gave them to her."

"Oh." I hadn't thought of that. "How do we prove it?"

"All this is going to take time. But I think we're on the trail. Just thought I'd let you know."

I had always believed that good eventually won out over

evil, but in court cases it doesn't necessarily happen that way. The burden of proof is on the person bringing the charges, I was finding, and not on the wrongdoer to prove his innocence. Or hers, in this instance. It seemed to me that the power of attorney was strong enough plus the affidavits we'd gotten, but apparently that is all "circumstantial evidence." And then there was Walter Jennings, who knew the local Virginia judge and the commissioner and the banker at the Jefferson Bank who could juggle the figures around. It seemed heavily weighted on their side, and I was getting more and more concerned about the legal fees and how I could continue to pay them.

The newspapers and magazines have articles now about the dangers of Halcion, the sleeping pills that Dr. Brady prescribed for Mother, and I'm beginning to wonder about him. Mother, who never took any pills and flushed antibiotics down the toilet, why was she being given Halcion at her age? Was that an attempt to confuse her mind, and then they could say that she was senile? Had Dr. Brady been in on the scheme with the others, helping her on her way, so they could get the money they were all so greedy for? At this point everything seems possible. How helpless really are elderly people who have money, not being able to trust anyone, as those around them wait eagerly for their demise.

A letter written in my head but never sent.

Dear Annabel . . . I often used to think that when we were older, as we are now and our parents are dead, that we would share memories of the family, of growing up together in the house on Tracy Place, maybe even travel together, to the Lake Country in England, where I've always wanted to go and is on my list of places not seen. But that will never be. You have ruined all that with your greed. You have destroyed everything that could have been.

But maybe you don't care. I wonder what goes through

your mind? I suppose you thought I would never find out that this wasn't Mother's real will, that you could just pull the wool over my eyes as you had in the past. You have hurt so many people. How can you live with yourself? That is the question that I want most to ask you.

How can you live with yourself, Annabel?

After Mother died and we were going through her clothes deciding which to give away, I found Kleenex in each of her pockets, in her jackets, her cashmere cardigans that she wore over her linen dresses, and it seemed so strange that now she was gone forever to find these handkerchiefs, as if she might need them at any minute.

"Did you find anything?" Annabel asked. She had given me the task of going through her clothes. Did she hope to find a diamond bracelet in one of the pockets or some other piece of jewelry? Mother had a habit of hiding things.

"No. Only Kleenex," I said.

"Oh, is that all."

Of course, as I later found out, Annabel had already cleaned out the safe deposit box and looked through drawers and in back of drawers in the secret place that Daddy had built to hide valuables from possible burglars.

But the main burglar he couldn't hide things from was Annabel, the "gimme gal" as he called her. How right he was!

I now find myself putting Kleenex in each pocket in case I need one. I wonder if after my death people will find them, and all the other things I cannot throw away. Mother had a habit of tearing up letters. Sometimes she would write to me, "Tear this up after reading it." Maybe she remembered going through her parents' things after their deaths and finding a photograph of an old lover that could cause pain. It was rumored that Grandfather had a mistress, though he and Grandmother remained married all those years. After his death a photograph was found hidden in the back of a closet by a new maid who was cleaning and innocently asked Mother, "Which member of the family is this?"

I probably should start tidying up, though I do not expect my demise any time soon. But one never knows. Are there things I would not want found after my death? It is just so hard for me to part with anything, dresses which no longer fit me, but recall happy times, hats I no longer wear in my casual California life, long white kid gloves once worn to a ball when we danced the tango and the Viennese waltz. I'm glad I lived in the era I did. Now I wear blue jeans to paint in, but I could never imagine wearing them out on a date, as the young girls do today.

Out of the blue there was suddenly a telephone call from Gillian.

"Aunt Barbara?" The voice was hesitant, worried, and my first thought was that something had happened to Annabel for her daughter to call me after so many years of silence.

"Yes?"

"Mother has been making a perfect fool of herself and I thought I'd call you to see if you could do anything. I hope you're not still mad at me."

"I was never mad at you, Gillian." After all, Gillian was my goddaughter and she wasn't responsible for what Annabel had done.

"Good, because I don't know where to turn."

"What is the problem?" It sounded like history repeating itself. "Though I've never had any influence with your mother, so I don't know how I could help."

"She's gotten herself involved with a man half her age and he's going through her money like water."

So there'll be none left for you, I thought. What Annabel

had stolen, someone else was stealing from her. Poetic justice. "Where did she meet him?" I asked.

"At a singles dance at the Sulgrave Club. He's a stockbroker and he's getting her to invest in all kinds of crazy things. Mother thinks Nigel is in love with her, but he just wants her money. And that's not all. My hairdresser knows him and he's gay. He has a boyfriend who works at an art gallery. What am I going to do?"

"I don't know what you can do, Gillian. Except hope that in time she sees the light."

"Suppose she marries him?" Gillian sounded panicky.

"I doubt that she will." But I wasn't so sure. Annabel could never stand being alone. "She probably just wants someone to escort her places."

"Oh, he's doing that all right. Including flying to Paris on the Concorde. Everyone is laughing at her."

The Concorde. I had never taken it but I knew how very expensive it was. Annabel was certainly traveling in style. I began to get angry thinking how she had stolen the money Mother had left Lavinia and Moses, who really needed it, as well as Todd, whose salary at the newspaper was barely enough to pay his rent, but at least he was working.

"I'll see what I can do, Gillian."

But I never called Annabel. What was the use? Annabel would do what she wanted to do no matter what, and nothing I said would make any difference.

So another Christmas passed with only silence between us and no exchanging of presents as in the past. I remember that when Annabel was married to Hugh I bought gifts for his two children as well as Annabel's three and seldom received a thank-you note. Mother asked me why I did it and said that they weren't family, only Annabel's children were, but it didn't seem fair somehow if they all didn't get a present from me.

Fair. What is fair? I feel as if I have been used and deceived and I have by trusting Annabel so implicitly. But it will all come around in the end. And that is what I am waiting for.

37

JUST AS I HAD ABOUT GIVEN UP, suddenly things started to happen. There was a call from Tim.

"I'm sending you an article from the *Washington Post* that I think you'll find very interesting." His words sounded less matter-of-fact than usual. "There was an audit of the trust department at the Jefferson Bank that turned up some irregularities and Lyle Percy has been accused of stealing from some of the accounts. He in turn has implicated Walter Jennings as his chief assistant in many of his crimes."

I felt jubilant. At last! "Then we'll get back what they've stolen from Mother's estate?"

"It will take a while, but I hope we'll recover part of it."

"Why not all?"

"It seems that Walter Jennings has already spent a good deal. He had a young girlfriend and took her to Paris and London and on a Caribbean cruise. When he dumped her she decided to talk to the IRS."

I thought of all the smug remarks Walter Jennings had made to me and how nasty he got when I asked for copies of Mother's previous wills, which he refused to give me, claiming attorney-client privilege. Now he was finally getting what he deserved.

"And what will happen with Annabel? Will there be a trial?"

"Oh, yes. She is definitely involved, though her name wasn't mentioned in the paper. But it will be."

What goes around, comes around. All of them tarred with the same brush. And yet, I felt somewhat sad. Why did it have to happen this way? Why had the money mattered so much to Annabel that she was willing to do anything for it and to hurt so many people?

"I'll keep you informed," Tim said. "But this should start to open up things."

After Tim hung up I sat staring out the window. How much would be left of Mother's estate after Walter Jennings had spent so much on a girlfriend? Not to mention Annabel's young boyfriend, who according to Gillian had gone through most of her money.

The idea of facing Annabel in court, my sister, did not appeal to me, but I supposed it would be necessary. I would have to testify against her, while she sat there with that sweet, innocent expression. Or perhaps she would burst into tears and accuse me of being a liar.

But none of that was to be, for Annabel had other plans . . .

38

IT IS ALL OVER NOW. Annabel is dead and there is a taste like bitter almonds in my mouth.

She was found by her housekeeper at the bottom of her swimming pool and the autopsy revealed a large amount of barbiturates in her body.

If only things had been different, if only she had not been so greedy. The Calhoun money never brought anyone much happiness. I think of Uncle Edgar. And my grandmother, who wanted to be an artist and didn't. Have I lived out her life for her, I wonder, and fulfilled her dreams? I am not Georgia O'Keeffe, but I have had personal happiness at moments in my life, and those memories remain with me.

Again I hear Daddy's voice in the library, the soft Southern accent tinged with bourbon reciting:

"It was many and many a year ago,
In a kingdom by the sea,
That a maiden there lived whom you may know
By the name of Annabel Lee."

We have played our parts and what has happened cannot be changed. The family album closes.

www.ingramcontent.com/pod-product-compliance
Lightning Source LLC
Chambersburg PA
CBHW031057020726
47495CB00007B/1918